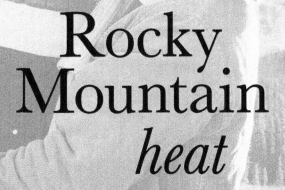

Rocky Mountain *heat*

Giulia Skye

Rocky
Mountain
heat

Cover design by Lori Jackson
Editing by Jenny Rarden

WANT EXCLUSIVE CONTENT AND SPECIAL OFFERS?

SIGN UP TO GIULIA SKYE'S MAILING LIST
www.giuliaskye.com

About the Author

Italian-born Giulia Skye spent her childhood watching classic Hollywood films and thinking up her own romantic scenes. After two decades working in TV production, she finally sat down to write them. Giulia lives in England with her husband and children. She still works in TV production but is at her happiest being a stay-at-home mum, growing her own vegetables, and conjuring up sizzling, page-turning stories about sexy, unique men meeting strong, original women when they least expect.

WANT TO HEAR THE LATEST IN GIULIA'S WORLD?
Sign up to her mailing list for exclusive content, bonus epilogues and special offers. She'd love to hear from you!
www.giuliaskye.com

To Howard Diamond

Thank you for being such a wonderful beta reader. I'm dedicating this one to you because you liked the story so much!

Chapter 1

"Oh, this is a really clever one." In the Banff Spa Resort's bar, Shane McDermit cleared his throat and read the glaring headline on his phone. "'The Nearly Man Nearly Makes it.' *Gah-faw*. Did someone seriously get paid to come up with that?"

Across from him, his good friend Michael Adams raised his beer in salute. "To media bullshit. May it live forever."

Shane chuckled. Mikey hated the tags the media had given them too. As pro swimmers competing for the same titles, they were reportedly enemies, with Shane the Nearly Man—*ugh*—who begrudged the Cocky Canadian—*that would be Mikey*—for beating him to the finish line every time.

Never mind that Shane was one of Australia's top athletes. Never mind that he'd won his fair share of races against Mikey. And never mind that when Mikey did win, it was usually only by the skin of his teeth.

"Here's another one," Shane said, tapping on the next article. "'In today's Icefields Parkway charity bike race, Australia's Shane McDermit *almost* made it across the finish line ahead of Canada's Michael Adams. But as per life in the pool...'" Shane raised an eyebrow. "*As per*? Why, this is some quality stuff." He sipped his beer. "'But *as per* life in the pool, Adams won by his usual fractions of a second.'"

"Fractions, eh?" Mikey shook his head. "It was a full two minutes."

"Now you're just rubbing it in."

Mikey laughed. "We all know you were out front for most of the race today. If it hadn't been for that collision when you made your pit stop, you'd've been ten minutes ahead of me. You made an awesome comeback."

"Funny how no one's reported that here." Shane tapped his phone.

"I don't know why you're even reading that crap."

Shane didn't know why either, but this past year, googling himself had become a form of self-preservation. The scars of the shit show back home in Sydney hadn't completely healed, and he never, ever wanted to be caught unprepared again. Not when his life had gone so tits up the last time he hadn't known what the tabloids were writing about him. Ever since, he'd taken control of what his fans and followers read. He often posted several times a week on his social media, generally leading the perfect life—even when he wasn't.

Putting his phone away, Shane leaned back with this beer, shifted in his seat, and winced.

"You too, eh?" Mikey said, also shifting in his seat.

"Flaming balls of fire." Shane grimaced for effect, making them both snicker like schoolboys. The race from Jasper to Banff had been a spectacular route, but three hours on a thin saddle hadn't done wonders for the family jewels.

"Hey, guys. What's so funny?"

Shane's gaze caught on skintight jeans then shifted up past a bare navel and the swell of breasts beneath a bright-blue crop top. Zoey Shaw.

"Hi," he said, a mixture of attraction and nerves swishing in his belly. She was the new fitness instructor at the aquatics center where he and Mikey trained, who—along with several others who worked there—had been recruited to help out on the bike ride. "How's it going?"

"Good, thanks." Her lips curled into a smile. "Are you guys sticking around to party?"

"Um. . ." Shane glanced at Mikey. Zoey and the rest of the team from the aquatics center had had the same idea to stay in Banff after the bike ride. Shane and Mikey had been invited to be part of their jolly group, but they'd opted to do a backcountry hiking and camping adventure instead. "Mikey and I are heading out to Lake Louise early tomorrow morning, but yeah, we'll stick around for a couple more drinks."

"Cool." Zoey shimmied her shoulders, which made her breasts jiggle a little. "I guess I'll see ya later, then."

"Feel free to go on after her," Mikey said when she was out of earshot. "I've gotta a few calls to make, anyway."

"Nah." Shane's gaze followed the sway of Zoey's hips as she joined her co-workers by the pool table then felt the weight of Mikey's stare on the side of his face. "What?"

"You had a date with her last week, didn't you?"

"It was lunch, not a date." Shane studied Zoey's ass as she bent to pick up the white ball out of the pocket. Unless he'd got it wrong, she'd been flirting with him for a couple of weeks and had been fond of stroking his arm whenever she was close enough. He'd never known a woman to do that before, but then, he'd been out of the game for a long, long time. Which was probably why he found her so tempting. But he'd moved to Vancouver six months ago as part of a new life plan. A plan that didn't involve any women. "You know I'm not interested."

With a crease between his eyes, Mikey studied his beer, and the word *Fiona* hung around them like a bad smell. "It's been a year, Shane."

"Yeah." Which was the other reason he needed this hiking trip. It fell bang smack in the middle of what would've been his and Fiona's first wedding anniversary—if she hadn't left him standing at the altar looking like a brokenhearted fool.

Shane took a long swig of his beer. His gaze followed the laughter coming from the pool table and landed on Zoey's breasts again then up her long, delicate neck as she talked happily with Ryan Dubois, one of the sports therapists who worked at the center.

"There's no harm in dating," Mikey was saying. "You might be ready for it now. Give it a go."

"Now that's some piece of advice coming from you." Shane shook his head and laughed. "Your schedule allows for women just as much as mine does."

"But I don't use it as an excuse if a woman catches my eye."

"Yeah—*if*."

"Hey, at least I don't pretend to be a hit with the ladies." Mikey shot him a pointed look, and Shane slid a little farther down in his seat.

So what if he only posted pictures of himself on his social media when an attractive woman was draped over his arm? So what if he made out that his life, when not in the pool or hitting the books, was one big party?

At least the folks back home could see he didn't give two shits about Fiona anymore.

Mikey's phone buzzed. "Aw, it's my dad. I'd better take this."

"Go ahead. I'll get another round of drinks."

Mikey stepped out, and Shane headed to the bar. While he waited to be served, his gaze strayed back to Zoey's pert backside.

Was Mikey right? Was Shane really ready to start dating again—for real?

And did he have the guts to find out?

"Two bottles of light beer and a glass of orange juice, please mate." Shane asked the bartender to put the drinks on his room account. Zoey was drinking orange juice. He'd surprise her with this next glass, start a conversation, and see where that conversation went. The other day at lunch, they seemed to have a few things in common—a shared passion for fitness, the same tastes in music and films—so maybe dating and hooking up with a woman wouldn't be so bad. . .

The bartender placed the drinks on the bar.

"Thanks." Taking his and Mikey's beers with one hand and Zoey's glass with other, Shane turned.

An elbow struck his hand, sending the juice splashing all over his face.

"Shit, I'm sor—whoa!"

There was skidding and clambering and a hand gripping his arm that almost made him drop the beers.

Krista Gervais.

Another sports therapist from the aquatics center who, every time Shane came across her, was always up to something...*interesting*.

Shane blinked juice out of his eyes and steadied Krista on her feet—well, not her feet exactly, but ridiculously high heels that had her legs splaying like Bambi on ice.

"Oh, man, I'm so sorry." Krista's face fell when she looked up into his. "Shane? I. . . um, are you okay?"

Orange juice dripped off his chin to join the wet patch on his shirt. "I'm just dandy, thanks. You?"

"Fine." She bit her lip, her brow creasing as her gaze traveled to his chest. "Your shirt."

"And yours."

"Wha—oh!" She gasped at the thin material of her pale pink blouse that was now wet and see-through across her cleavage, showing off the lacy bra underneath. "I. . . yeah, I'm just gonna go change!"

She shot out of the bar, her legs moving quickly and awkwardly, as if her ankles were tied together by those impractical shoes. When she reached the bottom of the stairs, she swung around. "I'm so sorry about your shirt."

"It's fine. Really."

"Right. Thanks." She pushed up her lips to what she probably considered a smile, mouthed the word *sorry* again, and then shot up the stairs.

The barman handed him a cloth.

"Thanks," Shane said. "I'll leave the beers here, and I'll be back in a minute."

"Sure thing."

Heading out the door to his room for another shirt, Shane glanced over toward the pool table. Zoey had her back to him, and no one had seen a thing. He'd buy her another drink as soon as he changed his shirt, but as he took the stairs two by two, he couldn't shake off the uneasy feeling that the spilled juice had been a big fat neon sign, flashing those same words he'd repeated to himself so many times this past year.

Stay away from women.

Chapter 2

THE DOOR HAD BARELY slammed behind her when Krista stripped off her sticky, orange juice–soaked top and tossed it on the floor.

Dammit! What the hell was wrong with her these days? Constantly running around like a headless chicken, bouncing from one embarrassing incident to another.

"Yeah, you're just *so* cool, Krista Gervais," she snapped at her reflection in the hotel mirror. "Way to go. And now you're talking to yourself."

She dropped onto her bed and buried her head in her hands. Man, she sucked at being cool and chic and—dare she say it in these modern times—*ladylike.*

Thing was, Krista was always one of the guys. Sweating out with them in the gym or carrying the beers and shooting pool with them after work. This was the first time she'd attempted to hang out with them in high heels and a pair of lacy panties constantly creeping up her ass. The combination of unsteady legs and itchy material where it really didn't belong was a world apart from the practical sports underwear she lived in. She slipped off her shoes. How the hell did women walk in those things anyway?

And of course, of all the people, she just had to crash into Shane McDermit.

She was still living down all the other times he'd caught her in an embarrassing situation. Like the time he'd walked in on her using the men's washrooms, and then a couple weeks ago, he'd witnessed her dropping a whole bottle of sanitizer, which by some freak chance cracked and spilled all over the sports therapy room floor, and then last Friday night. *Oh, god.* Her younger sister Lisa had rocked up at the center in tears with Deranged Duane behind her, and of course it had to be Shane who'd walked past just as Krista yelled across the parking lot, "Dude! Leave my sister the fuck alone. She's not into you!"

Perfect. Just perfect. What a truly professional image to flaunt in front of a star Olympic athlete. If she carried on like this, she'd be classed as a distraction. An amateur. A liability. And she wouldn't have a hope in hell of traveling with Team Canada to the next Olympics.

The ringing of her phone cut through her embarrassment. Lisa's name flashed on the readout.

"Go away," Krista said as soon as she connected the call.

"If you don't want to speak to me, why answer?"

"Because I'm curious about something," Krista huffed. "How the hell can you wear such uncomfortable underwear?"

"Aha!" Lisa hooted. "So you did pack them!"

Lisa had been horrified when she'd seen Krista's vacation underwear selection. But despite Krista's insistence that there would be no need for lace on this hiking trip, Lisa had been as persistent as ever. "If you want to get Ryan into bed," she'd said, "you'd better take these instead." She'd then dumped an armful of red and black lace on to Krista's bed. "Take your pick. And remember—dress to undress."

Good thing that she and Lisa were exactly the same dress size—or maybe not.

"These panties of doom are coming off." Krista scrubbed her face with her free hand. "And the shoes are already off. Thongs and high heels are not a good mix for me."

The proof? Crashing into Shane McDermit and a glassful of orange juice that she could still smell on her skin.

"As soon as you get into bed with Ryan, you can take everything off," Lisa said.

"Ryan likes me the way I am."

When Lisa stayed quiet, Krista frowned at what her sister was so clearly thinking—that Ryan saw Krista as one of the guys, too. Doubt echoed in the silence. If he really did like her the way she was, they'd have started a relationship weeks ago.

Damn.

Krista sighed, wishing she had an ounce of her sister's confidence with men.

Well, not men—just one man, really.

Ryan Dubois.

She'd been in love with him for almost a year. Newly single after her five-year relationship with Eric had finally fizzled out, she'd started working at the gym and had instantly clicked with Ryan. He'd shown her around, guided her through her first days. They'd taken lunch together then discovered they had so much in common that they quickly became friends.

Good friends. The best of friends!

Ryan confided in her all the time, especially these past few months as he dealt with the messy fallout of his parents' divorce. He'd supported his mother through her depression, and his personal life had taken such a battering recently that Krista was only too happy to be there for him.

You're my rock, Krista. How many times had he said that to her recently? *I don't know what I'd do without you.*

They'd been skirting around a relationship for months—and a few weeks ago, they'd even kissed on her couch, until Lisa had walked in with a guy she'd met at a bar.

Then fate had struck, and there hadn't been any more kisses after that. Granny had passed away, and Krista's life had become just as hectic as Ryan's. She'd had to deal with her grief, help her mom and Lisa through theirs, as well as sort through Granny's belongings and all the unpleasant paperwork that came with death. Ryan's mom had still needed a lot of attention, too, so he'd said they should wait for a better time before they started anything.

And that was exactly why Krista had suggested this mini vacation to Banff. When the center announced that they needed volunteers to support the athletes taking part in today's bike ride, Krista had signed herself and Ryan up. She'd then suggested that they spend the rest of the week in the Rockies. Together, alone. It was just what they needed to kick-start their relationship, exploring the trails—and each other.

Or rather, that had been the plan until Ryan had invited their co-workers to join them. Which meant they'd gotten separate rooms too, so as "not to spark gossip" and make things "awkward" in the group.

"All you've got to do, Kris, is bend over right under his nose," Lisa was saying on the phone now. "It works every time."

"If I bend over, half my butt will be on display." For god's sake, why was she even contemplating this ridiculous seduction plan? "These capri pants are so tight."

"They're supposed to be tight. They make your ass look great, and Ryan's gonna love it, trust me."

Trust Lisa?

Oh no.

Now, Krista really did feel desperate.

But the other night, when Ryan had come over to watch a movie, they'd almost kissed again, and Krista knew in her heart that now was the *right time* they'd both been waiting for.

Ryan's mom was finally getting professional help with her depression, and the drama of his parents' divorce was slowly being pushed to the past. And as for Krista, she still missed Granny, but at least the old apartment had been cleared out now, the sale had gone through, and she was no longer faced with daily reminders of her loss. Finally, she could move on with her life too—with Ryan by her side.

"Are you sure this'll work?" Krista asked, readjusting the lace panties out of her crotch for the hundredth time. "It feels kinda. . . prehistoric."

"Are you kidding me?" Lisa snorted. "If you think men are no longer into lace underwear, you most certainly need to get laid immediately."

Yeah. . . that would be nice. . .

It had been a very long time since Krista had been intimate with anyone. The kiss she'd shared with Ryan all those weeks ago had been the closest thing she'd had to bedroom action since Eric, and even the love life she'd shared with him, though sweet and comfortable, had never been. . . exciting.

"You and Ryan have been dancing around each other long enough," Lisa continued. "It's time to get down to business."

Lisa was two years younger than Krista, but in terms of notches on the bedpost, she was twenty years older. The heights of Lisa's wild love life weren't something Krista had ever wanted to aspire to. Picking up guys in bars, sleeping around, and "getting bored" if a man stayed too long? For sure, her party-girl sister was having a lot of fun sowing her wild oats, but all too often she ignored the warning signs that such a lifestyle could, and usually did, end in tears.

The main warning sign being Deranged Duane.

Lisa's ex-one-night-stand had several screws loose. Though at least Krista screaming at him like a crazed fishwife across the parking lot had done a good job of stopping his stalker ways.

Not that Lisa was remotely troubled by such a drama. *Dear god.* The next weekend, she'd gone out and brought home another loser. Just like Mom always did. But whereas Lisa seemed to embrace their mother's ways toward men and relationships, Krista didn't. At all.

Clearly, she'd missed out on the flirting, casual-sex gene that obviously ran down the female line of the family. Even Granny had had her fair share of male suitors, if the amount of old gentlemen who attended her funeral three months ago was anything to go by.

But nope. Krista wasn't anything like Lisa or their mom. She believed in monogamy and soulmates and ever-lasting love.

She believed in romance, dammit.

And above all, she believed that she and Ryan were meant to be together.

Hence, the *only* reason she was going along with Lisa's plan to seduce him with a scrap of lace.

"Ryan's gotten too used to having you in the friend zone," Lisa continued. "You've got to show him you're a woman with needs and you're not gonna wait around for him to make up his mind about what he wants."

"I know," Krista sighed, having heard all this from Lisa before—and her sister was right. Ryan did need to see her as more than a friend.

"You're wearing that short white blouse with the slit up the back, right?"

"I was, until I was doused in orange juice."

"How did—"

"Never mind." Krista pushed off the bed. "I'll wear that halter neck you loaned me." She pulled it out of her bag then bit her lip when she noticed the low-cut neckline. "What if this plan doesn't work?"

"There's only one way to find out, so grab the bull by the balls and show Ryan what you've got."

"It's horns. Grab the bull by the horns, not the balls."

Lisa cracked up. "Now we know where you've been going wrong all these years."

Chapter 3

CLEANED UP AND DRESSED in a fresh top, Krista adjusted the cups of yet another lacy bra Lisa had loaned her.

Grab the bull by the balls.

With one last look at her reflection, Krista was ready for *Meet Ryan at the Bar, Take 2.* And she had to admit she looked pretty good in skin-tight capris—even if she couldn't breathe in them. The low-rise waist barely reached her hips and didn't cover the lacy top of her panties. Neither did the hem of her black top, which left an inch of bare skin around her waist. Butterflies pounded in her stomach. She didn't look like herself, but she was on vacation now and it was party time. The whole point was to look different.

Boosted by her little pep talk, she headed across the lobby, her heels clicking on the shiny wooden floor as she followed the music and laughter to the bar.

Ryan was the first person she saw. Her heart raced.

"There you are," he said. His even white teeth flashed and his eyes sparkled as his gaze traveled up and down her body. "You look great!"

"Thanks." When he kissed her cheek, the scent of his newly shaven skin shot straight to her stomach. "You're looking pretty good too."

"It's a nice change not wearing sweaty sports gear, eh?" Ryan ordered a round of drinks, and together they carried everything toward the pool table, where the rest of their co-workers were racking up for another game.

Krista said Hi to everyone, and they talked about the day's race and bantered about the skill level of whoever was taking the next shot at the table.

When it was Krista's turn to play the winner, she reached for the cue and her gaze caught on Shane McDermit. In a clean shirt, he was talking to Zoey and Michael Adams at the bar. The tips of Krista's ears burned, but she ignored Shane's presence and took her shot at the table. Angling her cue, she pulled back her arm, and *whack*, the triangle of balls dispersed and one dropped into the top right pocket with a clunk. Her friends whooped and Ryan high-fived her as she walked past him to take the next shot. Feeling better, she bent over the table, positioning her cue, and—*gotcha!*—Ryan's gaze hooked on her cleavage.

Lisa was right!

A bit of skin really was the way to go. Ryan sidled closer.

"You've got this, Kris," he said.

Melting with delight, Krista took her shot and potted another ball.

"Hustler!" Darren, her opponent and fellow sports therapist, called out.

But she missed the next shot, and when Darren took his go, she took a swig of her beer. The alcohol tingled her senses and increased her confidence. Enjoying herself, she smiled at Ryan. He smiled back, and as he cheered her on throughout the game, she knew they would be together.

"Okay, *hustler*," Ryan said when she had one last shot on the eight ball. "You can finish this."

All she needed now was for him to stand behind her, because this last shot required her to really bend over, but he was hanging out by the pocket she was aiming for. Never mind. She'd get this ball in, win the game, and jump into his arms for a celebratory hug. Aiming her cue, Krista stretched back into her right hip, and—

Crrriiiickkkk!

A waft of cool air hit her bare ass. Her pants had ripped. Shooting up straight in sheer horror, she thwacked the cue against the white ball, which sent it flying across the table and knocking the eight ball into the top right pocket.

As everyone cheered—thank god all eyes had been on the ball!—Krista edged backward to the door, whooping and high-fiving as best she could with one hand behind her holding her pants together.

"Okay!" she said, plastering on a smile. "Now that I've beaten y'all, I'm just. . . um. . . gonna head upstairs. I've. . . er. . . gotta call my. . . my sister! I'll be right back."

Backing out into the lobby, she tripped and stumbled against the doorframe.

A pair of warm hands shot to her hips, steadying her.

Nope. Not a doorframe.

Twisting her neck, she looked up, and the blood drained from her already shriveling body.

Shane McDermit.

He must've seen *everything*!

Instinct had her desperate to jump away, but if she did, everyone would see her ass. So without a word, she clamped her hands over Shane's to keep them in place on her hips and pushed back into his groin.

"What the—"

"Keep moving," she squeaked, nudging him backward across the lobby until they were at the foot of the stairs.

For several long seconds, neither spoke. Until Krista realized that the ground wouldn't in fact swallow her up and suck her away into nothing.

"Well, um—"

"That was—"

"Yes," Krista snapped. Slowly, she straightened and went to move away, but something tugged her back. Reaching behind her to pull her torn pants together, her worst fears were confirmed. Threads from the ripped material had caught on Shane's fly.

"Jesus Murphy," she hissed.

Shane chuckled behind her.

"It's not funny."

"You're right," he said, his hands fumbling against hers as they both tried to free her pants. "It's hilarious."

Asshole. Krista swotted his hands away, twirled her finger around the caught threads, and snapped them free.

"Thanks for your help," she managed, and just when she thought the evening couldn't get any worse, she noticed Michael Adams a few feet away, watching the whole sorry show.

Beauty! Now she'd embarrassed herself in front of not one, but *two* pro swimming stars. If she kept this up, Team Canada wouldn't allow her anywhere near the Olympics.

Hauling a smile onto her face, Krista looked from Shane to Michael and back to Shane again, who was sucking his cheek, like he was trying—badly—not to laugh.

The jerk.

"Well, um, yeah. I'm just gonna. . . yeah. . ." She smacked her lips together then bolted up the stairs sideways like a crab.

Way to go, Kool Krista! Way to go!

"Did I interrupt something?" Mikey asked, his lips twitching.

"No. In its loosest form, that was actually me trying to help a damsel in distress."

Mikey snickered. "She kinda looked like she hated you."

"I have that effect on women," Shane said and strode out of the hotel by Mikey's side. "Some have even been known to run away from me."

"Not Zoey."

"Still with that?" It wasn't like his quiet-mannered friend to play matchmaker, but he knew Mikey's comments were a good-natured attempt at getting him to *move on*. Not many people outside of Australia knew about the messy state Shane had been in after Fiona, but Mikey had eventually found out. News had spread through the swimming grapevine when Shane had missed one too many training sessions because he'd got too drunk the night before with another nameless woman.

Yep, for a few weeks last year, Shane McDermit had become unrecognizable. Even to himself.

"All I'm saying is, Fiona screwed with your head," Mikey was saying now as they walked up Banff Avenue. "Everyone makes mistakes, everyone experiences a downward spiral once in a while, but you picked yourself up, brushed yourself off, and now look at you."

"Gee thanks, Pops," Shane drawled.

"Are you meeting Zoey later?" Mikey asked as they crossed the street toward the noodle restaurant they'd chosen. "Because I was thinking you should ask her to take my place tomorrow."

Shane stopped. When Mikey's dad had called earlier, it was to tell him to head back to Vancouver for a new sponsorship deal he'd just landed. The money from this deal would finance Mikey's training for the next couple of years, but he was hating having to forfeit the hiking trip. Shane didn't want Mike to feel bad about leaving him to hike alone. Maybe if he did ask Zoey to join him, even for a day or two, it would ease Mikey's conscience.

"Do you think she'd wanna come?" Shane asked, giving it some serious thought.

"She was all over you at the bar earlier, bud," Mikey said, "and it'd be a shame to waste those national park permits."

"Hmmm." Shane rubbed his chin. *But what if she said no?* "I'll think about it."

Chapter 4

PALE DAWN LIGHT SEEPED through the crack in Krista's blinds. For a blissful moment, she luxuriated in the warm comfort of her bed—until her stomach knotted with a ball of cringe. Her eyes flew open.

Her ass.

Exposed.

Shane McDermit.

And worst of all, she still hadn't had her time alone with Ryan.

After her stupid pants had ripped, she'd raced to her room to change, but once cocooned in the quiet privacy, she'd given up on the seduction plan that she was so obviously not cut out for. Ryan had messaged to say they were all heading out to dinner, but her appetite had gone and she was too pissed at herself to feel like joining them.

She'd also still been too annoyed and embarrassed to go downstairs in case she bumped into Shane McDermit again.

Wasn't he just one big flashing sign telling her to give up?

She ducked under the covers.

As soon as she got back to Vancouver, she'd shove that handful of pitiful lace back in Lisa's drawer.

Lesson learned?

Be yourself.

Ryan liked her plenty just how she was, didn't he? All Krista had to do was get a few minutes alone with him to talk, and she'd get that today. The hike they'd planned would take at least four hours, and even if the rest of their co-workers would be joining them, she was sure that they'd all walk at different paces.

With that in mind, Krista flung back the covers. Determined not to reflect on last night's disaster anymore, she dressed in her running gear, cleaned her teeth, and headed downstairs, ready for a hard, fast run to shift the last remaining strands of embarrassment.

It was early, and the hotel lobby was so quiet. Just as well. She didn't want to face anyone she knew right now, not until she got her head together. Stepping out of the front entrance, she set the timer on her wristwatch then skidded to a halt.

Shane McDermit.

He was standing next to his car, reading something on his phone. She ducked behind a potted plant then slipped off to the side of the building, just as Michael Adams walked out of the hotel toward him.

"All set, mate?" Shane asked, not having seen her.

"All set. Thanks for doing this." Michael patted the roof of the car and slipped into the passenger seat.

Shane got in, and the two Olympic stars drove off.

Thank. The. Lord.

Jogging off in the opposite direction, Krista puffed out her cheeks with the breath she'd been holding. At least she had a few days to recover from last night's *bare ass* display before she ran into McDermit again.

Ugh.

Her eyes squeezed shut at what he must've seen—her ass cheeks separated by a thin line of lace—no doubt wondering why she was even bothering to dress to impress. All her life, Krista had never felt comfortable dressing up. She was a Plain Jane. A pair of simple slippers, not dazzling, sexy stilettoes.

Desperate to outrun her embarrassment, Krista picked up her pace and headed down Muskat Street which the Banff map she'd studied earlier told her would lead to the quiet, mostly paved trail along the Bow River. Her footsteps pounded on the deserted sidewalk. Soon, she settled into her stride, finding freedom and solace in the quiet, empty streets.

Dawn broke across the sky. The surrounding mountaintops silhouetted by the pale light of a rising sun. She turned back toward town, toward the hotel, but took a wrong turn.

Damn.

Lost in her thoughts and her mistakes, she hadn't been paying attention, and now she struggled to get her bearings in the grid of unfamiliar streets. She stopped running. A sign for the Tunnel Mountain hike caught her attention. This was another Banff trail she'd researched and earmarked to do with Ryan, and she was right at the foot of it now. Still needing to get her head together, Krista followed the signs and a few minutes later reached the trail head. It was barely six a.m. The recommended time for the hike was three hours return, but her fitness level was good—she'd do it in two—and she could be back at the hotel in time for breakfast.

She marched up the trail and, an hour later, the streets and houses of Banff nestled below her and she was high enough to revel in the views of the mountaintops—an awesome, appetizing taste of the hiking to come.

Excitement flushed through her system. Ryan would love this view. Krista made a quick descent, running down most of the way. She couldn't wait to tell him about this dawn hike. Couldn't wait for them to set off on other trails together.

She couldn't wait to tell him how she felt about him.

When she arrived back at the hotel, almost three hours after she'd left it, she no longer felt miserable, embarrassed, or defeated. She felt fortified—ready and willing to grab that bull by the balls.

As she skipped through the hotel lobby, the smell of coffee and breakfast wafted around her. She headed straight for the stairs—ready to knock on Ryan's door, wake him up, and tell him *now* was the right time for them to be together—but as she placed her foot on the first step, her gaze snagged on the back of his head through the restaurant.

He was up already?

She followed his path to the hotel gardens.

"I'm here," he said.

Krista stopped dead. Ryan wasn't talking to her.

She was still a few meters away, and his back was to her as he stepped into the paved area, surrounded by potted plants and blooms. He raised his hand.

From behind a bush, long, slender fingers slipped into his palm, and Zoey stepped toward him.

What the hell was going on?

Krista shot behind the squat spruce trees, immediately feeling like she shouldn't be here, like this wasn't something she was supposed to see. She should leave. She should go to her room, shower, and change, but she couldn't tear herself away. Like a naughty child, she crouched in the shrubbery and peered at them through the branches.

Why was Ryan sitting so close to Zoey like that?

Their shoulders were almost touching, and their knees bumped against each other's. Then Zoey whispered something into Ryan's ear—something he obviously found so frickin' hilarious.

Why doesn't he ever laugh with me like that?

Zoey rested her hand on Ryan's thigh.

Krista sneered.

Not in a million years had she ever thought Ryan would fall for Zoey's flirty, hair-flicking ways. Not her Ryan. He was far too sensible and cautious.

But here he was now, with Zoey, and—*oh, my god*—he was stroking her back, and Zoey was tilting her face to his, and—*noooooo!*

They were kissing!

Krista covered her eyes.

No, no, no!

"Whatcha doin'?"

Krista jumped, the slow Australian drawl behind her scraping at her jagged nerves.

Shane McDermit.

What the hell was he doing back here? And why couldn't he just fuck off instead of always turning up at the most inconvenient, most embarrassing moments of her life?

"Who're you spying on?" he said.

"I'm not spying." Krista scrambled to her feet. "I was just... looking at something." She plucked a pine needle out of her hair and frowned, her pulse thumping in her ears. "I thought you'd already checked out to go hiking with Michael."

"Nah, Mikey had to bail. He's been called back to Vancouver for a sponsorship event. I've just come from dropping him off at Calgary Airport." Shane's gaze drifted over Krista's head to the gap in the trees, and his eyes narrowed. "Hey, who's that kissing... huh. Zoey."

At Shane's sharp tone, Krista looked up. Hazy work-place rumors of Shane and Krista having lunch last week jangled in her mind, as did the snapshot memory of them talking at the bar last night. "Are you and Zoey seeing each other?"

"No." But Shane's jaw hardened, and Krista wasn't convinced.

"The two-timing bitch," she mumbled out of spite and hurt.

"It takes two to tango," Shane drawled.

Krista's gaze darted back to Ryan. For sure, it didn't look like he needed any coaxing to lock his mouth with Zoey's.

"Are you and Ryan dating?"

"No." The hard fact of it was like a slap in the face. Red-hot rage boiled in Krista's stomach, propelling her past the solid wall of Shane McDermit. "But I'm still gonna give them a piece of my mind."

"Whoa! No you don't." Shane caught her hand and pulled her back into the bushes. "You'd better calm down first, Krista."

But this level of anger wouldn't cool down for days—*months!*—and Krista couldn't simply stand by and watch the man she loved be taken by another woman. She'd had enough of sitting around and being passive. If only she'd acted on her feelings weeks ago, she wouldn't be in this situation.

She went to move around Shane. His arm locked around her waist.

"Let me go!" she hissed, but he lifted her off her feet in one easy move. "Why, you! Let me go! I—" His hand clamped over her mouth, and before she'd had the chance to prize it off, he'd already carried her to the lobby.

"For god's sake, Krista! What the hell were you gonna do? Have a catfight?"

"Whatever it takes to get her off him."

"Don't be such a fool. Ryan was enjoying himself just as much as Zoey. If you're not dating, he's got a right to kiss any woman he wants."

The truth of his words hit Krista like a bullet to the heart. Pain hitched her breath, and hot tears stung her eyes. She sniffed and gritted her teeth, but her attempts to not cry were pathetic. Much like her.

And Shane knew it too. The way his lips curled in disgust made Krista want to crawl away and hide. How could she have lost it like that just now? In front of Shane. In front of *anyone*.

Crushed and beaten, she flopped onto the lobby chair and clutched her head in her hands.

"Aw, don't cry over that mongrel," Shane said. "He's not worth it. No one is."

"But Ryan. . . He's. . ." She sobbed. *He's my best friend. My soon-to-be boyfriend.* They'd shared so much these past few months. They had such a deep friendship. How could he kiss Zoey like that when. . . when. . . Krista had been there for him so much?

She wept harder, letting the tears pour of out her—loss, disappointment, and loneliness dripping onto the hotel floor—until a hard thigh nudged against hers. Shane was still sitting beside her.

Mortification plugged the leak of her tears. Krista gulped and wiped her eyes with the back of her hands.

"If it makes you feel any better," Shane said, "I came back to ask Zoey if she wanted to take Mikey's place on our hiking tour. I guess she has other. . . *things* to do now."

"It doesn't make me feel any better." Krista sniffed. "But how can you just sit there, not at all bothered that the woman you want is with another man?" *The man that I want!*

"Oh, I'm bothered all right." Shane's eyes turned hard. "But there are plenty more fish in the sea. One woman is much like another."

Yuck.

What a caveman thing to say. What a *Lisa* thing to say. Her sister thought all men were the same too.

But Shane and Lisa were wrong.

There was a special someone for everyone, and Ryan had been special to her. . .

Swallowing her hurt, Krista got to her feet. "I'd better go pack my bags."

Shane pulled her back. "Why?"

"Because I'm not hanging around here, watching those two love birds make gooey eyes at each other for the next few days." *Dammit.* Now she'd revealed even more of her true loser self to macho-caveman, *all women are the same* Shane. Her cheeks flushed. "I mean, I couldn't afford this resort anyway. If I check out now, I can still get some money back, and get someplace cheaper for a few days, and—why are you staring at me like that?"

"You take Mikey's place. Come hiking with me."

"What? Why?"

"Let's beat those two wankers to it and pretend we hooked up first."

"No way."

"It'll be six nights, Krista. Separate tents. I've still got all of Mikey's gear in my car and camping permits for two. Let's show Ryan and Zoey they never meant anything to us."

"Wha—hold up. You want to use *me* to save face in front of *her.*" *What a joke.* Zoey had red carpet looks, whereas Krista was more your average fireside rug—as last night's seduction techniques clearly proved. Who'd believe she'd hooked up with Shane McDermit, anyway? He was on Team Elite, and she was on Team Nobody. "It's a stupid idea."

"C'mon. Give it a go. Camping will be cheaper than any hotel around here, and you want to make Ryan jealous, don't you?"

"For sure, if I were sixteen and still in high school." Krista shook her head. "I don't play games."

"Why not? Games are fun." Shane shot her a pointed look, as if she didn't know the meaning of the word. "And I hate to break it to you, but judging by your reaction to what he's doing with Zoey right now, it looks to me like that guy's been playing games with you for a long time. And so has Zoey with me." Shane stood and towered over her. "Isn't it about time we played a game of our own?"

"What do you mean?"

"I mean, if you like the guy, show him you're not gonna wait around forever. He'll soon be at your feet."

That's exactly what Lisa always said, too! Shane really was her sister's male equivalent.

But growing up, their mom had constantly played games with men—she probably still did with live-in lover number six—and as for their father. . . He was going through divorce number four. Forever changing bed partners wasn't how Krista wanted to conduct her love life. Ryan had shared Krista's need for steady, deep relationships. That's why she'd always agreed with him when he'd said they should wait for that elusive *right time*.

Huh. Looked like the right time had come for Ryan. . . but not with Krista.

"C'mon," Shane was saying. "The sun is shining, the sky is blue, and there're all those lakes, mountains and hiking trails to explore."

The hiking. That's what she'd wanted to do all along, wasn't it? But not with Shane.

Just then, Ryan's and Zoey's laughter cut through the air. Shane pulled Krista into a recess, and Ryan and Zoey walked by hand-in-hand, completely unaware that they were being watched.

Krista snarled at their retreating backs.

"Don't get mad, get even," Shane chimed next to her.

Out on the sidewalk, Zoey's raven-dark hair reflected the early morning sunshine. When she tipped her head back, Ryan swooped in to kiss her again.

A bolt of anger swamped Krista's pain.

Ryan doesn't want me! Ryan doesn't care for me!

If he did, he wouldn't be sticking his tongue down Zoey's throat.

"All right, Shane, I'll do it." She pushed away from him. "Now, let's get the hell out of here before I throw up."

Chapter 5

BACK HOME IN SYDNEY, Shane's mates always said he had an excellent poker face, and he was deploying it now while he and Krista waited their turn to check out of the Banff Spa Resort. Mouth relaxed, breathing steady, gaze loose, he took in the minutiae of his surroundings—the sparkling hotel reception desk, the log trim, unlit fireplaces. The stack of leaflets advertising day hikes and tours. Krista's red eyes, pursed lips and puckered brow.

Yeah, I get it.

Seeing Zoey with Ryan had given Shane the same stab of disappointment, but unlike Krista, who looked like she'd had her heart slammed against a brick wall, annoyance and betrayal fueled Shane's irritation.

Zoey had led him on with those lingering glances and the bright smiles she'd flashed his way at every opportunity. At first he'd kept things polite and professional between them, brushing off Zoey's attention as simple friendliness. After all, he'd come to Canada to get away from women—or, rather, one woman—and didn't need or want the distraction of a relationship. But when she'd asked him out to lunch last week, it had seemed rude to refuse.

And then came her *friendliness* last night. Hell, she'd come on strong enough when they'd talked at the bar, hadn't she? Stroking his arm again and leaning into him. Even Mikey had noticed.

"She's into you, buddy," Mikey had said again during dinner. It was that observation from his friend that had pushed Shane over the edge in his decision to ask Zoey to come hiking. And considering she had been showing signs of being interested in him, Shane had been dead cert that Zoey would say yes.

Looks like you've been fooled again, idiot.

Which served him right for ignoring his new life plan. He should've stayed clear of women. . . because now he was all het up and rejected and hurt, feeling all the things he'd never again wanted to feel.

Bad memories of how he'd been last year, almost to the fucking day, gripped his gut and threatened to undo the mental balance he'd worked so hard to regain after his life had been derailed by Shitstorm Fiona.

But why had Zoey led him on like that?

Had she used him as bait to get Ryan's attention? Just like Shane was now suggesting Krista should do?

Krista was right. This whole stupid plan to set off hiking together and pretend they'd hooked up first really did smack of high school antics, and a good dollop of hypocrisy, too. But after Fiona, Shane had vowed that he'd never again let a woman get the better of him, which meant he was only too happy to brush Zoey off like a piece of lint on his jacket and show her that she meant as much to him as he did to her—a big, fat nothing.

And he believed Krista should do the same with Ryan.

That's why Shane had dragged her away from starting a catfight. He hadn't wanted her to do anything she'd regret later. God knew, Shane regretted enough himself. He'd absolutely fucking lost it over Fiona! Turning up at her door pissed out of his skull, sobbing his bloody guts out, skipping training session after training session. His whole world had crashed. Publicly. Humiliatingly. *Everyone knew. Everyone saw.* And not even his poker face could mask the pain.

For weeks he'd crawled through the rubble of his life until he could no longer bear all the sympathetic head tilts his friends and family were constantly giving him.

Poor Shane. He looks like shit.

Poor Shane. He was so happy.

Poor Shane. He always misses out.

So Poor Shane upped and left the country. He'd transferred his training and post-grad studies to Vancouver—and devised that new life plan. A plan that had no room for a woman to fuck it all up for him. And yet, he'd let his guard down with Zoey, foolishly falling for her dazzling smile and deep-green eyes. Beckoning. Enticing. Her sweet words about getting to know him better so intoxicating.

What a load of bullshit.

"Excuse me?" Krista turned to him.

Had he said that out loud? Shane cleared his throat. "I meant this swanky resort. I'd much rather be in a tent."

"Me too." With folded arms and a sulky mouth, Krista looked to the floor again. "My original idea for this vacation was to camp in the national parks."

"Why did you all book into this place, then?"

"We had a group vote, and the majority wanted luxury—and no mosquitoes." She shrugged. "I'd planned a whole bunch of day hikes with. . . Never mind."

Ryan.

The blush on Krista's cheeks told Shane that she'd been about to say his name. He'd often seen them together at the aquatics center canteen or leaving work in the evening. The assumption that Krista and Ryan were a couple had always wafted at the back of his mind. He hadn't taken much notice really, but now, Shane fit the pieces together and saw the whole. Krista was in unrequited love.

It was so obvious by the pain in her eyes. Had she been expecting to do more than just hiking with Ryan? Was that what last night's dressing up in heels and flesh-flashing clothes had been about? The image of her ass through the split in her trousers pinged in his brain. Recalling the strip of red lace, Shane scratched his chin. *Well, yeah.* It certainly looked like Krista had been hoping for sexy times with Ryan.

Just like Shane had been hoping for sexy times with Zoey.

He shook the thought away now.

Silly bastard.

When would he ever learn that women weren't worth the pain?

THIRTY MINUTES LATER, OUT on the road driving toward Lake Louise, Shane glanced at his new hiking companion.

She'd barely said a word since leaving the hotel and was now sitting rigid in her seat. Shane could practically feel her vibrating with all that restrained rage and injustice rioting in her eyes.

If only he could get the message across that affairs of the heart—or however else people referred to them—meant jack shit. One year on from his own heartbreak, he wasn't that beaten up, soft-hearted loser anymore. He should hang on to that as a reminder that he'd never wanted to return to that state ever again.

And for the brain cells at the back, that means staying clear of women, got it?

Sex could be good—most welcome, actually—but love was a waste of time.

In fact, the new, level-headed, optimistic part of him would even go as far to say that Fiona had done him a favor.

He'd dodged a bullet when she'd called off their wedding.

And he'd certainly dodged a bullet catching Zoey pashing off with Ryan.

Getting hitched, being tied down? No, thanks. *Having a girlfriend whine about him spending too much time in the pool?* He'd pass.

No one but him put demands on his time. He was the captain of his own ship.

But too bad that ship currently contained a passenger whose face could sink a whole fleet.

Hoping to snap that scowl off Krista's face, he asked, "Ever been to Lake Louise before?"

"No."

"That makes two of us. You wanna do the lake shore trail first then head up to the Big Beehive?"

"Sure."

"I'd like to hike up to Lake Agnes too and try out that teahouse I keep hearing about. You up for that?"

"Yes." Krista turned to the window, but that constant crinkle on her brow was still there, irritating the hell out of him.

"Did you tell your friends at the hotel that you were leaving with me?" he asked.

"Yes. I texted Ryan too."

"What did he say?"

"Nothing yet. I guess he's got other things on his mind." Her bottom lip quivered. "Did you text Zoey?"

"Nope." Shane's curt word cast an even darker shadow over Krista's face, but what more could he say? He didn't owe Zoey an explanation. He didn't owe her anything. Although, he liked to think that his impromptu take-off with Krista had put Zoey's nose out of joint. Just as he intended.

But enough about Zoey.

"So you're all good with doing the hikes I planned to do with Mikey?" When they'd left the hotel, Shane had handed Krista the details of the hikes he'd researched and where they'd be camping these next six nights. Krista now had the trail maps and leaflets on her lap. Shane had seen her look at them, but she had yet to comment. "Don't feel like you have to do the longer hikes though. We've got some tough ones planned, but you could do the shorter circuits."

That got her sitting up—just as he'd hoped.

"I can handle the distance," she said. "And the elevation and terrain. Don't you worry about that."

Meaning—don't treat me like a dainty flower.

Now that he knew she had buttons to press, Shane sucked in a cheek. "Well, I'm taller than you. I'll need to adjust my pace to suit your slower one."

"Oh, I'll match your pace, Mister Hot Shot. Hiking's my thing."

It was his too. The Canadian Rockies offered some of the best hikes in the world, which only made Shane more irritated with her. If Krista loved hiking so much, why had she gone with the majority vote and opted to stay in the hotel? From what Zoey had told him last night, the only hikes the group had planned were the ones around Banff. Picturesque, yes, but there were so many stunning trails beyond the town limits. Obviously Krista wasn't the captain of her ship, and that pissed him off. Was she so in love with Ryan that she put his wishes before hers?

Now that really bugged him, because once upon a time, he too had been so in love that he'd bent to each and every one of Fiona's wishes—lavish nights out, the city apartment, a pedigree toy dog that always yapped at him, a big fancy car, and the big, fancy white wedding. . .

Krista's phone bleeped, saving him from revisiting that well-trodden, bitter road down memory lane that led exactly nowhere. He glanced at Krista as she yanked her phone out of her bag and stared at the screen.

"Ryan?"

"Yes."

"What's he say?"

"He wants to know if I'm okay. He's confused as to why I've gone hiking with you, and he's asked if I'll be back on Sunday for the flight home."

"Did he mention Zoey?"

"No." Krista's shoulders sagged, and Shane had that urge to shake her again.

"Love sucks, Krista," he snapped. "The sooner you accept that, the better."

Chapter 6

UGH. SHOULD'VE KNOWN HE'D be a love-sucks kinda guy.

But as Shane parked the car in Lake Louise's main parking lot, Krista couldn't be bothered to tell him that he was wrong.

Love was awesome.

Love made the world go round.

Love was. . . not what she had with Ryan.

Ouch. She recoiled as the truth slapped her in the face again.

She'd been an idiot. All these months, she'd been a muppet. A pushover. A donkey hankering after the carrot Ryan was forever dangling in front of her nose.

Just let me get over this shitty time, Kris. . .

I want us to wait for the right moment. . .

We can't start anything now. Life's too complicated. . .

There was always *something*—and she hadn't even realized it. She'd let herself be brainwashed into a state of limbo. They were neither a couple, nor just friends, and Krista had trotted, willingly, after him.

She stared at the message he'd sent her. Sure, he asked if she was okay. Sure, he cared that she'd still make the flight back home.

But why no mention of Zoey?

As Shane parked the car at Lake Louise, Krista texted Ryan back:

Shane made me an offer I couldn't refuse.
You know I've always wanted to hike the
Rockies. See you Sunday.

He replied:
OK.

Krista stared at her phone. *Okay?* That's all he had to say?

She switched her phone off and shoved it into the glove box. Shane cut the engine, and she got out of the car, gripping the handle so hard her knuckles turned white as she fought the urge to slam the door and kick a dent into the side of it.

Instead, she marched across the parking lot, ignoring the monstrous Lake Louise hotel that dominated the view to her right. She focused only on the peaks towering beyond the lake, struggling to see anything past her hurt and anger. Behind her, Shane hummed a jaunty tune she only vaguely recognized. She lengthened her stride to get some distance from him, pushing past her fatigue from her early morning run and hike up Tunnel Mountain.

Love sucks. The sooner you accept that, the better.

What the hell did he know about love?

Nothing, from the sounds of it. His quick dismissal of Zoey had left Krista feeling cold. Clearly he wasn't an emotional man.

One woman is pretty much like any other.

And weren't those just the words of a guy who slept around? Who always let the little head below override the big, empty one above.

Ryan wasn't a guy like that. He didn't flirt or have one-night stands, which was why Krista was having such a hard time dealing with what she'd seen him do with Zoey this morning. Ryan and Zoey were friends. All their co-workers were friends. They had a great workplace environment, but. . . where had his feelings for Zoey come from?

So many times, Krista had lain next to Ryan on the bed or the couch, watching movies, talking—often until late at night—and only once had they kissed.

Now, that didn't sound good, did it? Kissing only once. She'd waited patiently for a sequel, but all she got was an endless prologue to a relationship that had never actually happened.

A knife twisted in her heart.

"Hold up!" Shane called out.

Krista whirled around. Several meters behind her, Shane was taking photos of the ice-blue alpine lake that flared bright amongst the dark pine trees and gray rocks surrounding it. She looked around her and rubbed her eyes. *What?* They'd hiked this far up already?

Squinting against the dazzling sky, Krista studied the snow-capped mountains that stretched for miles around them. Man, she'd ached to see these views. Ached to be on the mountaintops, in the clouds, amongst the tips of tall pine trees. She'd craved to see it all with Ryan, to share the experience with him, but now, so tangled up in her thoughts, she'd turned blind to it all, unable to get the image of him kissing Zoey out of her mind.

"Oh, for fuck's sake," Shane hissed beside her. "Guys like Ryan aren't worth shit, so stop torturing yourself."

Krista blinked. "I'm not. . . not. . . torturing myself. I was just thinking."

But the wobble in her voice betrayed her, as did the tear rolling down her cheek. She sniffed and wiped her eyes, mortified that she was again crying in front of Shane.

"You want hearts and flowers, sugar and spice and all things nice? Well, it's bullshit." Shane's eyes narrowed as he sucked in a breath. Krista braced for more harsh words, but the air whooshed out of her instead.

Shane had wrapped his arm around her shoulders and was pulling her tight against his big, hard body.

"Remember what I said about making Ryan jealous?" he said. "It's time to turn that frown upside down, Krista. Smile!"

Too stunned to do anything else, Krista stared at the phone Shane had raised in front of them, and *click*—he took a selfie.

"Gorgeous," he drawled, releasing her as he looked at the phone. "I guess that sort of passes for a smile." He tapped the screen a few times and showed her what he'd done. "That's up now."

What?!

Krista stared at the Instagram post on Shane's phone. The expression on her face in the photo didn't pass for a smile at all! But neither did she look anywhere as near as upset as she felt. She looked...stunned and dazed. Exhilarated, even. Like she'd been plucked out of a comfortable bed and dropped bang, smack in the middle of a big, amazing adventure.

That was all okay, except—

"We look like we're. . . we're. . . together!"

"That's the whole point, remember?" Shane slipped his phone back into his pocket. "Your Ryan will be knocking at your door in no time."

"Oh, for god's sake. He's not my Ryan, and he's not some teenage boy who'd get jealous over your silly game."

"Wanna bet?"

"For sure." Hysteria had her laughing. "A hundred bucks says you're wrong."

"Deal." Shane slapped his hand into hers.

What the—"Seriously?"

"A hundred bucks says your precious Ryan is a man with an ego. When he gets a whiff that you've moved on, he'll be sweeping you off your feet, confessing his undying love for you."

"You're an idiot if you think that." Man with an ego or not, Ryan wasn't interested in her. This morning had proved that. Hell, the past few months had proved it too. But Krista could do with a hundred bucks, and proving Shane wrong would be the cherry on the goddamn cake. She stared down at his large hand in hers and squeezed. "Game on, McDermit."

Chapter 7

ALRIGHTY. SO, MAYBE POSTING a picture of them together on his social media wasn't the smartest move, but Shane hated that love-shattered look in Krista's eyes. He'd seen it plenty of times before—every time he'd looked in the mirror during those first few months after Fiona had jilted him—and he couldn't stand Krista moping around any longer. But if it helped distract her and shift those storms clouds thundering above her head, coughing up a hundred bucks in a stupid bet would be worth it.

"Also, it's not your place to post photos of me on social media," Krista was going on behind him like she'd been doing for the past ten minutes. "Now everyone'll think we've hooked up!"

"That's precisely the point," he said, also like he'd been doing for the past ten minutes. She was right of course. He really should've asked her permission before posting that photo, but they had a deal now. She'd said it herself: *Game on*. "We're showing Zoey that she didn't mean anything to me, and we're trying to get your Ryan jealous."

"I told you, I don't like playing games, and he's not *my* Ryan, and besides, he'll be too busy screwing Zoey to care about me hooking up with the likes of you."

"Then you'll not only have a hundred bucks, but you'll also know, once and for all, how he feels about you."

Her eyes were lit with fury. *Good*. Anger was a good sign—at least she wasn't crying. He hadn't liked those tears earlier. He'd shed enough himself and knew firsthand how pointless they were.

Had crying ever changed anything for him?

Nope.

He'd still been jilted. Fiona had still trashed his heart and soul. And the worst part? While he'd been crying over his loss, she'd wasted no time shacking up with another guy.

So, no. Tears weren't worth the effort, and neither was churning up the past.

Hating that Krista's misery was bringing back memories of his own, Shane picked up his pace. Twigs and stones crunched beneath his feet as he tried to lose himself in the craggy, rocky landscape. But soon, the wildflowers and the sun glittering in the icy mountaintops had him drifting to the Snowy Mountains back home where, three months before their wedding, he'd taken Fiona there for her birthday weekend. The Snowy Mountains were just as vast and pretty as these mountains here. They'd hiked and talked about their *big day* and had lain side by side, naked in bed, thinking about their future together.

Yep.

That was so-called love for you—one big, fat lie.

But Krista obviously didn't think the same way, so Shane would play along with their stupid bet and do all he could to make that idiot she was infatuated with jealous. Anything to cheer her up. He didn't want her misery to drag on his energy and ruin his holiday.

Shane glanced back at Krista now. Head down, eyes fixed to the ground as she walked, still looking pissed off. *For god's sake*. If she was going to be like this for the next few days, Shane would rather take her back to Banff and set off by himself, although he couldn't do that now he'd posted that stupid photo on Instagram. Krista couldn't face all those questions from her friends alone, especially in front of Ryan and Zoey. She'd be humiliated, and that hadn't been Shane's intention at all.

He should delete the photo before anyone had a chance to see it, but as he pulled his phone out to do just that, Krista walked alongside him, her eyes glassy, her jaw tightly clenched, and her shoulders bunched around her ears.

Oh, good Lord. That's it! No more.

The stupid bet clearly hadn't been enough of a distraction.

"I have a question for you," Shane said, planting his hands on his hips. "You had the hots for Ryan, yeah? You thought he was your Mr. Right? So why didn't you tell him how you feel? What were you waiting for?"

"It's none of your business."

"I wasn't asking for my benefit. As long as you know the answer, that's all that matters."

Krista stopped in front of him. "Well, if you must know, I did tell him. Sort of. And I was gonna discuss it with him again today, only—"

"You had to discuss it?"

"That's what friends do, isn't it?" Mirroring his stance, she planted her hands on her hips too. "And not that you'd understand, but life's been stressful for him lately. He needed a friend, so I was there for him."

"The poor love," Shane said, pouting like he used to as child when he wanted to bug his older sister Claire. "Did he have a boo-boo and need some TLC?"

"Like I said, you wouldn't understand." Krista cocked her head. "You don't believe in love, so it figures you're also *That Guy* who thinks men who show emotions are weak."

"Actually, I think men who string women along are weak. Maybe he just liked having you around, like an emotional crutch."

"An emotional crutch? Is that what you think Ryan saw me as?"

"This may come as a shock to you, but I really don't think about Ryan at all." Shane barely knew the guy, but up until this morning—when he'd clearly shown such little regard for his friendship with Krista—he had always seemed decent enough. Although, there was one thing that always niggled Shane about Ryan. Whenever he came across him at the aquatics center, Ryan was usually in front of a mirror in the changing room, preening his hair. Once, he'd even caught him smoothing out his eyebrows. Each to their own and all that, but Shane couldn't relate to that level of self-grooming.

"So you and Ryan weren't a couple," he said, continuing to bug her. "You were waiting for whatever you were waiting for, and now you're hacked off because another woman got there first, baby. Deal with it."

"Don't call me baby," she hissed.

Shane swallowed back a smile. He shouldn't be pushing her buttons like this, but Krista was wound so tight trying to keep her shit together that maybe letting loose was exactly what she needed. The sooner she got the venom out of her system, the sooner he—*they*—could both enjoy this trip through the Rockies. If directing some of her anger and frustration toward him helped, then so be it. Otherwise, Shane really would be dumping her back in Banff as soon as they got off this trail.

"Tell me," he said. "What is it about that pretty boy that had you so hooked like a fish?"

"A pretty boy? A fish? Jeez, but you're an asshole, McDermit."

"Aw, I'm just curious as to why women find him so attractive." Shane stifled a chuckle. "I mean, his face is okay if you like cleft chins and chiseled cheekbones, and of course, those lush waves of his hair are styled to perfection. And as for those eyebrows. . ."

"What about his eyebrows?"

"Does he pluck or wax?"

"Ugh." Krista rolled her eyes and shoved past him. "I think you should shut the hell up now, don't you?"

"Sure thing, *baby*!"

She flipped him the finger.

Shane burst out laughing then hung back as she marched along the trail, keeping to a blinding—and rather impressive—pace.

Yep, burn that anger off—baby!

Shane sniggered. Clearly, he hadn't forgotten those finely tuned little brother techniques at annoying the hell out of people, even if it had been a good twenty years since he'd had to use them. Next time he spoke to Claire, his sister, he'd have to tell her all about it, though Claire was sure to message him the moment she saw his Instagram post with Krista. *Ah, shit.* He hadn't thought about that. Mum and Dad would be curious too. His family always grilled him about the women he posed with. Always eager for him to "move on" from Fiona with a "meaningful relationship" and "settle down" with a "nice girl."

Never gonna happen, folks.

Shane scrubbed his face then pulled out his phone to delete the Insta post. But of course, if his family, friends, and followers back home saw this, there was a high chance that Fiona would too.

Zoey wasn't the only person who Shane wanted to show the world meant nothing to him. Constant photos on social media of the new love of his life—having a ball in the Canadian Rockies with his pretty Canadian lover. . . Was there a better way to *celebrate* the week that would have been his first wedding anniversary?

Shane stared at the photo of himself and a shell-shocked Krista then pocketed his phone without deleting anything. What was the harm in leaving that photo up for another few hours?

And he did have a bet to win, too. Shane was certain that someone as vain and needy as Ryan Dubois would sit up straight when he saw another man's arm around Krista, a woman he must've assumed would always *be there* for him, thinking the sun shone out of his arse.

Shane picked up the trail again, catching up with Krista. She'd covered a good two hundred meters without him, and he hoped to hell that his plan of annoying the misery out of her had worked.

But what if it hadn't? What if he'd made things worse?

You'll soon find out, mate. . .

A few minutes later, Shane approached her with caution as she sat on a slab of rock overlooking Lake Louise. Expecting that she'd still be shooting daggers at him, he primed himself with a few more leg-pulling quips.

"Feeling better now, *baby*?"

She whirled round. "Call me baby one more time, and I'll throw you off the mountain."

"Okay." His hands shot up in surrender. "I'm just kidding, you know."

He sat next to her on the rock, and for several long, peaceful minutes, they sat listening to the wind softly whistling in the trees.

Then Krista groaned and mumbled something. Something that sounded like a lot like, "You're right."

Shane frowned. "Right about. . ?"

"Ryan. We shouldn't have needed to discuss our relationship. It should've just happened. I'm such a fool."

"We're all foolish sometimes," Shane said. He plucked a long blade of grass out of a crack in the rocks. "Don't beat yourself up about it."

"It's hard not to," she said, resting her chin on her knees and leaving Shane no choice but to tickle her ear with his piece of grass. She swatted him away. "God, you're annoying."

Sniggering, he got to his feet. "Up you get, Krista. Any more of this flaming heart-to-heart crap, and things will be dropping off between my legs. I'll be turning from a rooster to a hen and singing Mariah Carey by the time we reach Lake Agnes."

"Wow." Krista squinted. "Sexual stereotypes must be all the rage in Australia, eh?"

"Nah." He pulled his most serious, most professional face. "I'm one of a kind."

She blinked. Once. Twice. Then rolled her eyes at his nonsense.

But he'd caught it, that quirk of her lips. Not quite a smile, but a vast improvement on the scowl she'd been wearing all morning.

Chapter 8

SHANE MCDERMIT WAS EXTREMELY annoying.

But he was also rather cunning.

As Krista followed him on the trail to Lake Agnes, the sneaking suspicion took hold that the sly joker had goaded her on purpose and turned himself into a punching bag. Why else would he have riled her so much one minute then been surprisingly gentle the next?

And why else would he have come up with that ridiculous eyebrow waxing comment?

What a douche thing to say.

Despite her state of turmoil, Krista fought off a smile and studied the pro swimmer with a newfound curiosity. He was keeping to a steady pace in front of her. Like all the athletes she worked with, his back, butt, and legs were solid and carved and were a reminder that, as an Olympian, he had drive and ambition and discipline.

And all he'd seen of her was a clumsy, short-tempered stress-head who'd split her pants and hid in bushes to spy on the guy she crushed on. She didn't even want to think about how she'd cried in front of him.

Good Lord.

"You must think I'm a total loser," she blurted.

Shane slowed his pace as he glanced over his shoulder at her. "Actually, I happen to think you're pretty kick-ass."

"Shut up." Krista snorted. "You're just saying that because you're scared I'll burst into tears again."

"Maybe." A soft smile curled his lips. "But it's true. You've got a kick-ass streak in you. I saw it the other night when you shouted at that poor bastard in the car park."

She winced. *Kool Krista strikez again.* "Yeah, about that. . ."

"I was about to step in to help, but you'd sent that guy packing well enough on your own, and I figured you'd bite my head off if I came near you."

"Wise man." Putting Duane in his place had felt good, but seeing Lisa so upset had gotten Krista in one hell of a foul mood. "I was beyond annoyed that you caught the whole sordid show, so yeah, I probably would've gone for your throat, too."

"Who was he?"

"My sister's ex." Krista sighed. "Lisa's in competition with our mom for the Who Can Fall for the Most Unsuitable Man award."

"Interesting contest. Who's winning?"

"It's too close to call. Mom's on live-in partner number six. He's a guy called Jonas, who has no job and hangs around the coffee shop she works at all day." And, man, didn't saying the words out loud make Jonas sound like a total loser? Which he was, but apart from the lack of employment and chronic laziness, he was harmless enough. Just. . . what the hell did Mom see in him? "And as for Lisa? Well, I had to threaten Duane with the police before he backed off, so that'll tell you how she's doing."

Krista stopped walking. Shane had pulled out his phone to take photographs of the lake through the trees, so while he busied himself with the settings on his phone, she stretched her legs and tried, unsuccessfully, not to think about his Instagram post.

Had anyone seen it yet? She'd ask, but she couldn't bear Shane thinking she was obsessed with Ryan. Not that she could blame him for thinking that, but she was feeling a little better now that she'd let off some steam in Shane's direction. Whether he really had goaded her on purpose or not, being with him had helped. The jagged mountains, the meadow flowers, and the sound of spruce trees waving in the wind had also helped. Her mood had brightened, and the shock of seeing Ryan and Zoey together had receded.

For sure, she was still pissed at Ryan for not telling her about Zoey, but she was even more pissed at herself because the clues that Ryan wasn't into her as much as she was into him had always been there. Only, she'd chosen to ignore them.

Don't beat yourself up about it.

Shane was right.

Who knew he'd be so perceptive?

Krista watched him again as he took more photos of the landscape, tapping buttons on his phone. What was he doing? Adjusting the light and focus? He was so immersed, so absorbed, so thorough. *That's the kind of mentality you need to succeed.* That kind of mentality that gets you to the top of your game.

The kind that she'd been missing lately.

"So, anyway, that night with Deranged Duane?" she said, feeling the need to give Shane some context to her behavior so he didn't think her completely cuckoo. "Thing is, Lisa likes to party. She has a couple of cocktails and flirts with any guy who takes her fancy. Duane being one such guy. I warned her that his *attentions* were bordering on stalker territory, but she didn't listen. Not until she tried to end it and *he* didn't listen." Krista puffed out her cheeks, the worry for her sister coming to the surface. "It's not like Lisa is defenseless or helpless. It's just. . ."

As Shane continued to take photos of the wildflowers along the edge of the track, Krista tried to find the right words to explain how she felt about Lisa's love life without coming across as either bitchy or jealous.

"You see, Lisa and I live together," she continued. "A couple years ago, we had enough of Mom's boyfriends moving in and out, so we found a place downtown. Lisa was twenty-two and I was twenty-four, so it felt right to move out anyway, and I think Mom was secretly pleased. We all get on a lot better now, so that's something."

Leaning against a tree, Krista took the weight off her tired legs.

"I really love our new home," she continued, "and I love my sister. I just wish she didn't bring guys back all the time. But at least when she does, I can keep an eye on who she's with, eh? I don't mind looking out for her. I mean, she's my sister, right? But sometimes. . ." She trailed off.

Shane's attention had been caught by a butterfly perching on a blade of tall grass by his feet. He took a photo of it, not remotely interested in her babbling on about her life. Why would he be? They were surrounded by this stunning scenery, and she'd already sucked up enough of his patience today.

She took her water bottle out of her bag and waited quietly for him to finish taking photos. If they were going to be spending the next week together, alone in the wilderness, it was important that she respect his privacy and boundaries. And knowing when to shut the hell up wasn't one of Krista's strong points.

"But sometimes. . ?"

"Eh?" Krista paused the bottle halfway to her lips.

"You were saying, you don't mind looking out for your sister, but sometimes. . ?"

"Oh!" Shane really had been listening. "Um. . . well, sometimes, it's hard to relax at home when she keeps bringing deadbeats back. It feels like it did living with Mom, so I took on more clients at the gym, but working longer hours—"

"—is exhausting too?"

"Yes." *Yes, it was.* "And these past few months, we've also been so busy dealing with my grandmother's estate. She died in January."

"I'm sorry."

"Thanks, but it's okay. Grandma had a very good life, but figuring out what to do with all her stuff was difficult." These past few months had indeed been busy, unbalancing, and Krista was not only tired, but also stressed and tense. Was it any wonder that she'd gone so batshit when she'd caught Ryan and Zoey kissing? She'd had no energy reserves to deal with that kind of disappointment. "I guess I just need a break."

"Well, here we are." Shane put his phone away and smiled at her. "Take a holiday, Krista, and treat yourself. Sounds like you've had a rough few months. You work hard. You're a good person. You need some time out."

"Thanks." She smiled back at him, his kind words smoothing the frayed edges of her sadness. They also confirmed her suspicions that he really had goaded her on purpose.

They continued to walk toward the teahouse. The sun was high and bright, so warm on her face.

Take a holiday.

That had been her plan all along. A couple-y vacation with Ryan, and when he'd asked their co-workers to come along too, she'd totally, idiotically, missed the big fat clue telling her coupley wasn't what Ryan wanted. Not with her, anyway.

And the irony? Everyone now thought Krista *was* on a coupley vacation—with Shane, thanks to his Instagram post.

Speaking of which. . .

She couldn't resist it any longer.

"Has anyone reacted to the photograph of us?" she asked, uncomfortable that by *anyone*, Shane would clearly know she meant Ryan.

"I haven't checked." And he seemed in no hurry to get his phone out to do so, either.

Then his quick dismissal of Zoey this morning came back to mind. "You didn't post that picture solely on my behalf to make Ryan jealous, did you? You posted it as a big *screw you* to Zoey."

Shane kicked a pebble as he walked. "Yeah, but in all honesty, although I was annoyed with Zoey this morning, I don't much care now what she thinks or who she's with."

"Over her so soon?"

"Nothing to get over. I'm not losing sleep over one lunch date and a handful of flirty chats."

"It was more than that with me and Ryan though," Krista said. "I thought. . ." *That he'd be the love of my life. That we'd be together and have babies and live happily ever after.* "I thought he cared for me."

"And I'm sure he does. Just not in the way you want him to."

Krista considered this. She'd let her crush rule her life these past few months, often changing her plans to fit in with Ryan's so she could be close to him. But that hadn't been Ryan's fault. Sure, he could've made up his mind about her sooner, and he certainly should've told her about Zoey, but Ryan was a nice guy—he wasn't a Duane—and they did get on well as friends.

But could she ever be just friends with Ryan?

Now was the time to accept that possibility, and like Shane had said, it was time to move on.

She didn't want to make Ryan jealous. She just wanted to have her *holiday*. She wanted to enjoy herself.

"So you're not worried about what people will think about *us*?" she asked.

"No, why should I be?" Shane stopped abruptly and turned to look at her. "Would our so-called hooking up make problems for you with your manager?"

"There aren't any rules about dating co-workers or clients if that's what you mean. As long as everyone acts appropriately, does their job, and doesn't bring the center into disrepute."

Shane nodded. "So, we're all good on our bet?"

"You're still serious about that?" Krista rolled her eyes. "Okay, so let's make it five hundred bucks, then. "

"Five hundred bucks is big talk."

"Because I know Ryan." At Shane's pointed look, Krista shook her head. "All right, maybe I don't know him as well as I thought I did, but I do know *me*." And her light didn't shine as bright as Zoey's. Ryan had made his choice. Krista couldn't compete.

And to her great surprise, neither did she want to.

"THEY'VE BEEN SERVING TEA here since 1905," Krista said as she read from the teahouse menu. It was a cute log cabin perched right on the shore of Lake Agnes. She'd insisted on buying Shane a midafternoon supper of soup and crusty bread. It was the least she could do after he'd done so much for her. They ate in comfortable silence then ordered two Golden Monkey teas, just because the name sounded fun.

As the waitress busied herself with cups and saucers, Krista eyed the cakes on the counter. They looked so gooey and decadent, particularly the double chocolate velvet layered one with cream on top. She licked her lips.

"And a piece of that cake please," Shane said next to her.

Krista looked up. "Man, I was looking at that, too."

"I know. It's for you."

She opened her mouth to protest, but Shane held up his hand. "Just eat the cake and enjoy it. You're on holiday, remember?"

The waitress placed their coffees and a huge slab of cake on the table.

Krista's mouth watered. "Okay," she said. "This'll be my vacation treat." She asked the waitress for another fork. "But you'll have to help me eat it. It won't be as much fun on my own."

Shane sighed heavily as he shook his head. "The things I have to do to cheer you up."

"Hey," Krista choked on a laugh. "I'm cheered up already."

Which was true. Her mini vacation may have started out crappy, but she was determined for it not to end crappy.

Fun would be the theme for the next few days. She'd take time out. Treat herself. Eat cake and enjoy the views—and not think about anything or anyone who had the power to drag her spirits down.

Krista forked up her first bite, popped it into her mouth, and practically melted into its heavenly taste. It was divine. She took another bite, and then another, and as she worshipped and *hmmm-hmmm'd* every mouthful, Shane ran through his suggested schedule for the next six days.

"So, tonight, we camp at Lake Louise, and then tomorrow, after we hike the Iceline Trail at Yoho Valley, we'll move out to the backcountry."

Another forkful of cake melted on Krista's tongue, and she closed her eyes to savor it.

"Then after Yoho, we do Emerald Lake, the Cory Pass, and Mount Edith Circuit. Thursday, we could either do Cascade Amphitheatre or the Bourgeau Lake and Harvey Pass."

With every bite, stress oozed from Krista's shoulders, like the chocolaty cream in her cake oozed every time she pressed her fork into the sponge.

"Then we could tackle the Grand Sentinel or the Paradise Valley and Giant Steps." Shane looked up from his trail maps. "Are you listening to me?"

"No. You've lost out to a slice of cake. Sorry."

Shane huffed, but his lips were twitching. He helped himself to a forkful then picked up his tea. "Wearing chocolate suits you."

"Eh?"

Shane tapped his upper lip.

"Oh!" Krista snapped out of her blissful sugar-daze and wiped her mouth, though no embarrassment rose out of Shane seeing her with chocolate smears on her face. It wasn't like this was a date and she had to impress the guy across from her. And Shane had already seen the worst of her, anyway.

Which was. . . very liberating.

She licked chocolate sauce off her lips and enjoyed every last crumb of her vacation treat.

Chapter 9

THE TUG IN SHANE'S groin as he watched Krista eat cake wasn't uncomfortable, just. . . unexpected. Those groans and moans and that blissful look on Krista's face as she'd closed her eyes, savoring each mouthful, had been way too much of a reminder of what he'd been missing lately.

Well, more than lately. It had been eleven months since he'd had sex.

Often, he didn't mind going without. His new life plan kept him too busy, but. . .

He missed getting naked with a woman.

A fact that Zoey had brought to the forefront of his mind last night. He'd even bought condoms this morning in case she'd said yes to hiking with him—in case *he'd* had the guts to ask her—and his mind had raced with possibilities of the two of them in the wilderness. . .

What a lucky escape he'd had!

The lure of sex had clouded his judgement. Hadn't he learned from his past mistakes?

The one-night stands he'd had trying to rid Fiona from his heart still left a nasty taste in his mouth. Despite how he came across on social media, casual sex like that hadn't ever been on his agenda. But now that *A Relationship* was top of his list of things to avoid, no-strings sex would be the only sex he'd be having for the rest of his life. And that kind of sex only came with the mutual understanding on both sides that *A Relationship* between would never appear on the horizon.

"Ready to head back to the car?" he said.

Krista nodded as she sucked her top lip, where another smear of chocolate had sat for the past five minutes. He would've told her about that one too, but she'd been enjoying herself so much, like she was—*yeah, like that*—and he hadn't wanted to interrupt her until she'd. . . *um*. . . finished.

Who knew a simple slice of cake could put such a blissful sparkle in those wounded hazel eyes?

"Hey, how about another photo?" he asked. "I've got a bet to win."

"Dream on." Krista wiped the corners of her mouth, the napkin not hiding her sly little grin. "I'll happily take your money though."

She shifted next to him, and with the mountains behind them, Shane took another photo. This time, Krista was properly smiling, and she looked good with it too, especially against the dark, alpine landscape and deep-blue sky.

"This will get your lover boy begging," Shane said as he posted it, along with a brief description of where they were.

"I wish you'd stop calling him that." Krista's smile faded. "You'll ruin my chocolate-induced epiphany moment." When Shane cocked his head, she pointed to her empty plate. "Thanks to my calorific vacation treat, I've decided to only suit myself from now on, especially when I return home. I won't be a shoulder to cry on anymore for Ryan. Zoey can listen to his problems now. So, you know what this means?"

"What?"

"Ryan really *was* using me as an emotional crutch. Which means"—her lips curled in disgust—"you were right, McDermit."

"Don't sweat it, Krista," Shane said in his most sympathetic tone. "Soon, you'll realize I'm always right. About *every*thing."

Eyes wide, mouth open, Krista stared at him.

He stared back, deadly serious. Until she whiffed the nonsense that had just come out of his mouth and cracked up laughing.

Her smile brightened her whole face again, and Shane took another photo of her.

"Hey," she said. "You're not gonna post that too, are you?"

"Not unless you want me to. I just thought you might like it. I'll send you all my photos afterwards if you want."

"That'll be awesome. I'm not one for taking pictures. I always seem to forget or never have enough time."

"Speaking of time," Shane said, putting his phone away. "We'd better head back to the car and make the most of Lake Louise campground. It'll be our last night of luxury for a few days."

"By luxury, you mean showers, right?"

"Showers, toilets. And sinks for our washing up after dinner."

Krista swung her legs around and stood. "Did you and Michael Adams actually plan to cook?"

"Of course we did," Shane said, heading back to the trail. "I don't think Mikey's culinary skills are much to write home about, but mine are. And nothing beats a camp stove meal."

"Having just had the best cake ever, I beg to differ."

"That cake has nothing on my world famous, one-pot sausages and beans."

"World famous, eh?"

"You're in for another treat."

Krista skipped beside him. "I can't wait."

Sitting at their campground table, Krista stared at the plate of blackened *sausages* that Shane had just placed before her. What might have passed for beans in another universe were also black and shriveled, and what she assumed had once been the tin of tomatoes she'd seen Shane pour into the saucepan now looked like lumpy black gravy.

"Eat up," he said, standing by the little stove he'd rigged on the ground. He spooned up a mouthful, and she was both horrified and surprised that he didn't gag. "Hmmm, it's come out *really* good."

And it had smelled *soooo* good, too. She'd thought the chocolate cake would've ruined her appetite for this first campground meal, but the aromas coming from their pitch when she'd returned from the washroom had been irresistible. How could Shane have ruined it so badly?

It had gone cold too. She hadn't been in the shower that long, but her meal had already congealed. She poked at it with her spoon. It looked like a bowl of sticks and stones floating in red mud.

Hold up a minute!

It *was* a plate of sticks and stones floating in red mud.

She looked up, and Shane burst out laughing. "Bon appetite!"

"You're such a jerk." But Krista couldn't help cracking up too. She picked a twig out of the bowl and flicked it at him.

"Your face!" he said, still snickering like a schoolboy. He placed a new plate and spoon in front of her and joined her at the table. "It took you longer to suss it out than I'd thought. You have so little faith in my cooking, huh?"

"Busted. But that totally looks like real tomato sauce in there."

"That's because it is. I accidentally knocked over half a can of it. I was annoyed to have wasted it, so I thought I'd make use of it anyway and have a little fun."

The aroma of a steaming bowl of sausages and beans in a rich sauce drifted up her nostrils. She tucked in and tasted her first mouthful.

Chili and garlic and tangy tomato zapped her tongue. "Shane McDermit, you have skills."

She hadn't known what to expect from Shane, though he'd seemed very confident and at ease setting up their camp. As soon as they'd checked in and located their pitch, he'd erected both tents and laid out his cooking gear and ingredients in less than half an hour. He'd declined all her offers of help, and sensing that he might've wanted some time alone, Krista had wandered around the campground instead, exploring the facilities and the views.

The campground buzzed with activity, so different to the Banff Spa Resort. This was the Rocky Mountain experience she'd imagined, and the fact that she wasn't sharing it with Ryan didn't seem to bother her as much as it had a few hours ago.

Over him so soon?

The true test would be when she saw him again, but right now, Krista remembered her promise. She was going to enjoy herself. She was going to relax. She was going to have fun.

"This really is delicious," she said, scooping up another bite. "Where did you learn to cook?"

"I just picked it up over the years. My parents are both foodies and often let me help out in the kitchen. Plus, I like eating. I was interested in learning to cook my favorite foods."

"And here's me thinking Aussies lived off barbeques."

"Oh, we do. Nothing like a good barbie, mate," he drawled.

"Do you miss Australia?"

"Sometimes. But I'll be home in six months when my post grad is finished, just in time for Christmas."

"Right, I heard you were only in Canada for a year." She'd also heard other rumors. "Is it true that you're thinking of retiring from pro swimming after the next Olympics?"

He stirred the food around on his plate. "It's been on the cards for a while."

"Do you think you'll miss competing when you give it up?"

"Life is always full of competition," he said evenly. "You should see some of the guys on my course. They study with jetpacks up their backsides and could give any athlete a run for their money when it comes to being competitive." He shook his head as he chewed. "Studying has never come easy for me. It's why I loved spending so much time at the pool when I was a kid."

"Oh, I loved school," Krista said, spooning up more beans. "I was the swotty one whose hand always shot up to answer questions."

"I can picture you, sitting up straight in your chair. I bet you had pigtails too."

"No, Lisa and I had ponytails. With ribbons."

"Of course." Shane laughed and ate some more. Swallowing his next mouthful, he added, "I'm dyslexic, so studying takes me a little longer than some people."

Krista lowered her spoon. "I didn't know that."

"Why would you?"

"No reason." She shrugged then took another bite of Shane's comforting meal. There was a lot they didn't know about each other, and yet here they were, on a mini vacation together, having a surprisingly good time after such an awful start. Her gaze drifted to the bowl of sticks and mud.

Shane noticed. "Want another helping?"

"Of the real stuff?"

"What else?" He winked at her. "Jokes are finished for the night."

"Glad to hear it." But there was something suspicious about that wink.

Especially when accompanied by the flicker of a mischievous smile.

·♥·♥·♥·♥·♥·

A COUPLE OF HOURS later, the campground quieted and every night-time rustling could be heard.

After cleaning the dishes, Krista had called Shane to the edge of the campground, away from the few lamps that lit the walkways, and they'd sat on a log to look at the stars. Moonlight shone off the ice on the mountain peaks as they'd talked—casual chitchat that had been comfortable and easy—and then they'd grabbed their washbags to get ready for bed.

"See you in the morning, Krista," Shane said as he unzipped his tent.

"Thanks again for everything. Despite the drama of this morning, today has been fun." She smiled at him. "Good night, Shane."

Krista crawled into her tent.

She'd already set up the thin inflatable mattress and the sleeping bag that belonged to Michael Adams. It was strange using his stuff, but no stranger than anything else that had happened to her today.

Placing her flashlight down, Krista dressed into her pajamas—the cozy kind, just like her. The lace underwear Lisa had bought her was firmly at the bottom of her bag, never to see the light of day again.

Dress to undress.

Huh.

Cozy pajamas it is, then.

And Krista was fine with that. It was the first step to accepting who she was, of doing only the things that pleased her, not others.

She pulled her T-shirt over her head, grabbed her flashlight—and yelped.

A frog! On her sleeping bag!

She shot away from it, clambering against the side of the tent. The canvas walls shook and. . . the creature flipped on its side, its stiff legs in the air. She shined her flashlight on it and saw it was a toy.

"Damn you, McDermit!"

Shane's soft chuckles drifted to her on the nighttime air. That wink he'd given her at dinner made sense now.

But as her pulse steadied, a smile twitched her lips. She snuggled down into her sleeping bag, holding the little wooden frog in the dark, then quickly drifted off to sleep.

Chapter 10

Shane had been up since dawn, enjoying the early morning peace, when he'd made the mistake of checking his phone.

Just as he'd suspected, the photo of him and Krista had generated a lot buzz on his social media. Though he never quite knew what that buzz entailed exactly, it was clear from the amount of reactions and comments he'd got on his post that quite a few people were assuming and speculating that he and Krista were now *something*.

He skimmed the comments. Most were nice and complimentary, a few weren't, but balls to those wankers out there who had nothing better to do than troll. It was time to take down the posts of him and Krista anyway. He'd been thinking about it last night. Now that they'd got to know each other better, and yesterday had turned out to be fun, he'd rather drop that whole ridiculous bet thing they had going. Shane really couldn't give a monkey's if Ryan came to his senses or not. Krista was better off without him, and after her so-called epiphany moment yesterday after eating that cake, it seemed like she knew it too.

And as for using Krista to show Fiona he was completely over her? Shane was feeling pretty pathetic that such a thought had crossed his mind in the first place. He was over Fiona. He didn't care what she thought or what she was doing. Yesterday his annoyance at Zoey and his abrupt change of plans had rocked his new life balance, that was all.

He was just about to delete his posts when he noticed a message from his sister.

`Hey, Worm, do you mind telling me who this one is?`

Claire was referring to Krista, of course.

`She's just a friend.`

Shane sent his reply then began to type out a longer explanation, telling Claire that Krista worked at the aquatics center and had taken Mikey's place on the hiking holiday. Knowing his sister, she'd get a kick out of the bet too.

`The photos are to make the guy she's in love with jealous, which means if you believe we're a couple, the money is already mine.`

He sent his reply, but as Claire lived in Sydney—near Mum and Dad—and being 17 hours ahead, she'd be asleep now and wouldn't see his message for several more hours. Just as well. Shane didn't want to deal with her concern that he was sleeping around again.

As if he would.

He may have gone off the rails during those awful weeks after he'd been ditched, but he'd soon come to his senses. He'd cleaned up his act—and ensured *he* was clean and healthy too. But it was hard shaking off his self-disgust at having one-night stand after one-night stand in futile attempts to dull the pain Fiona had caused.

How could he have been so reckless?

And how could he have treated those women so carelessly? He didn't believe for one minute that any of the women he'd slept with had hopes for a relationship or that he'd left them brokenhearted or even done anything against their will. But to discard them as soon as he'd used them? It was unforgivable. And most definitely not the type of man he was or ever wanted to be.

The Bad Times gripped his soul. Shane immediately switched his phone off and reached for his coffee. He took a sip and then another.

Nope. He wasn't going to regurgitate what had happened a year ago.

Fiona was in the past. He may have turned into a bastard on the rebound for a few drunken weeks, but that too was in the past. Today was a new day, and Shane was focused.

Focused on his training. Focused on his studies and on the end goal of a new career after he retired from pro swimming.

And right now, he was focused on relaxation, enjoyment, and untangling his mind from uncomfortable memories.

But still. . .

As he watched day break over the mountains, echoes of *this time last year* rankled in his head.

Him, alone and humiliated, in a church side room having just been told that Fiona wasn't coming. . .

"Is that coffee I can smell?"

Krista's voice shattered his memories. Shane turned to face her, and—*good grief, what was she wearing?*

And what else had he expected?

"Cute jimjammies," he quipped as she crawled out of her tent in stripy pajama bottoms and a top that was covered in fluffy kittens.

"Go ahead and laugh," she said, sticking her chin out. "Pajamas are warm and practical."

"Of course they are. I have several pairs myself, for when it's too cold to sleep in the nuddie."

"In the nud—" She held up her hand. "Actually, don't elaborate."

Shane swallowed back a smile.

"It's the actual kittens I'm objecting to, anyway," he said. "They're so. . ." Turning up his nose, he waved his hand in the air as he thought of the right words. "Sweet and fluffy."

"Well, I like sweet. I like fluffy."

"Yeah." He poured her a mug of coffee from the flask he'd made. Steam rose in the cool morning air as he handed it to her. "I bet you used to draw love hearts on your schoolbooks, too."

Krista nodded proudly and sipped her coffee. "I also dotted my I's with them."

Of course. "My sister did the same. Her love hearts were puffy and round. I used to tell her they looked like upside-down butt cheeks."

"Delightful boy."

"I guess there's a reason why she nicknamed me the Worm," Shane said, snickering. "So, how did you sleep?"

"Like a baby. You?"

"Same."

Krista held up the little wooden frog he'd found on the back seat of his car—having got it a while back with some promotion from his local supermarket—and placed it on the table. "Your little friend kept me company."

"He's helpful like that. It's why I keep him around."

"I should've known you still played with toys," she muttered with a smile then turned to gaze at the mountains through the trees of the campsite. "So, yesterday was a very interesting and very long day, eh?"

Krista looked thoughtful, and no prizes for guessing what—or who—she was thinking about.

Ryan.

Shane drew breath to tell her that he was going to delete the photographs and that they should forget their stupid bet. Forget social media, too, and everything else except the Rocky Mountains. But then she yawned and stretched out like a lion.

"Man, I ache," she said. "I must've covered over twenty kilometers yesterday, what with my run along the river and hike up Tunnel Mountain."

What? Shane lowered his coffee. "You did a hike *before* we left the hotel?"

She nodded and yawned again.

"Wow, Krista, we're meant to be relaxing, not killing ourselves."

"Exercise does relax me."

"Yeah, I get that." But then he recalled how he'd ribbed her yesterday morning about not being able to keep up on the hikes. "You know I was kidding about you taking the slower options, don't you?" He could tell straight away that Krista wasn't afraid to use that compact body of hers. Not that Shane had dwelt on the firmness of her butt and thighs whenever he walked behind her, or the muscle definition in her arms and shoulders. He'd just happened to notice, that was all. "I know you're fit. I was just trying to get a rise out of you to cheer you up."

"That annoying chauvinist act was you being nice, eh?" She narrowed her eyes at him. "I actually figured as much afterwards, though Lord knows how."

Shane chuckled. "Because I'm full of charm and chivalry."

"Well, you're full of something, for sure," she drawled, eyes sparkling. She sipped her coffee, and just like that, all the bitterness and hurt that had seeped into his bones a few minutes ago had been flushed back to the past where they belonged. "Why are you looking at me like that?"

"Huh? Oh!" Shane blinked away his surprise at the effect Krista was having on him. "I, um, I was thinking about the Iceline Trail. If your legs ache, we can do a shorter hike today if you want."

"Are you kidding me? I can't wait to do it. I might ache, but after yesterday, a six-hour hike will be a breeze. Unless, of course, *you* can't handle it."

"I can handle it."

Amused—and impressed by her enthusiasm—Shane got up to get breakfast ready.

"I'm going to the washrooms," she said.

"You do know the rest of the world calls them toilets, right?"

She wrinkled her nose as if he'd said something vulgar. Shane laughed, and again he was surprised by how quickly his mood had shifted.

Well, he was surrounded by mountains and fresh air, and the excitement of another day's hike was coursing through him. That in itself was more than enough to kick the Bad Times away.

Whistling, he mixed milk powder with water and placed the jug on the table, along with a bag of cereal, two bowls, and two spoons. Waiting for Krista to come back, he necked the rest of his coffee and almost choked when something hit against his top lip.

He stared into his cup then burst out laughing at the little wooden frog he found at the bottom, soaked in coffee.

THE IMAGES KRISTA HAD seen on the internet of the Iceline Trail were stunning, but nothing could ever have prepared her for the real-life experience.

They started their hike from the Takkakaw Falls parking lot, having decided to tackle it in a clockwise direction. This meant they had a thigh-screaming hour of steep switchbacks to climb, propelling them a 1000 meters higher, but the view of Takkakaw Falls across the valley had been more than worth the effort. A little farther along, when they'd cleared the tree line and reached the moraine plains, the views opened up in every direction. There were mountain peaks, deep valleys, and dozens of glaciers.

The terrain had changed from the soil of the forest floor to sun-bleached, frost-bitten rocks. Patches of snow and ice clung to cracks and crevices, and slithers of meltwater twinkled in the sunshine between their feet as they walked.

"It's so pretty here," she said, letting out a deep breath. Fresh mountain air cooled her throat, and the sun heated her skin. *This* was exactly what she'd wanted from her vacation, and now that the shock and heartache of Ryan and Zoey—and all that shit—had melted away from her soul like ice and snow among the rocks, she was really enjoying herself.

This was turning out to be a perfect day.

Shane stepped up beside her. "Are you ready for lunch?"

"I'm always ready for lunch."

They wandered a little off the main trail to sit on a huge flat rock overlooking the valley.

Shane handed her a paper bag containing the cheese sandwich he'd made this morning, along with an apple and a protein bar. "Here are your rations until dinner."

"Gratefully received, thank you."

They ate their sandwiches in companionable silence for a while, listening to the birds and the gentle trickling of a meltwater stream.

As she unwrapped her protein bar, the meals that Shane had prepared came back to mind—from muddy sausages and beans, to this morning's breakfast of canned fruit and cereal, to this packed lunch. Shane had even thought to bring paper bags to wrap everything in. "I'm still surprised you came so prepared with supplies."

"I was in the Scouts for many years," he said. "I'm always prepared, especially when it comes to food."

"A Scout, eh? There really is no end to your talents." Krista took the last bite of her protein bar and hugged her knees. "You're a handy guy to have around in the backcountry."

Tonight, and for the next three nights, they'd be camping somewhere off the Icefields Parkway toward Jasper. It wasn't strictly backcountry, but wild and remote nonetheless, with only the most basic of facilities. Krista was part excited, part nervous. She loved sleeping outdoors, she loved the wilderness, but the city girl in her couldn't help but be a little apprehensive of such primitive isolation. And after all the hiking she was doing, a long hot soak in a bath at the end of the day would've been awesome.

An idea struck her.

"Shall we go to the Miette Hot Springs one day? They're not far from Jasper."

"Absolutely. Maybe we can go on the last day, and then we'll head down the Icefields Parkway again, back to Banff."

"Awesome," she said. "I didn't get to see much of the Icefields Parkway on bike ride day." Her sports therapy station had been at the halfway mark, and she, Ryan, and the rest of her co-workers had all piled into the organizer's minivan as soon as they'd gotten everything packed up. Everyone had had their sights on partying back at the hotel, and Krista. . . well, she'd had her sights on Ryan. "You still okay to get me back to Banff by noon Sunday?"

"Of course." Shane stretched his leg in front of him and studied his foot. "How do you feel about catching the same flight home as Ryan and Zoey?"

"The other guys from the gym will also be on the flight. They'll most likely be asking me what hikes we did. . . and whatever else we got up to here, thanks to those photos you posted." She shot him a pointed look.

"Ryan will be all over you by Sunday. I reckon he's already ditched Zoey, or Zoey's had enough of him, and your Ryan would've figured out he's been a fool and realized it's you he wants."

"You have a wild imagination," Krista said, shaking her head. "I almost feel bad for taking your money when you lose the bet."

Of course, she wouldn't take Shane's money, but carrying on with this bet was amusing. It also made her feel in control, that even though she'd been upset and disappointed by Ryan, she was still able to joke about this whole random scenario.

But Ryan falling at her feet in a fit of jealousy? No way. Shane was a sweet guy to think it would ever happen, but Krista couldn't imagine it.

They packed up their lunch bits and continued their hike. They crossed half-frozen streams and soon absorbed themselves in the mountains, stones crunching underneath their feet and virgin-white clouds bundled against the vast blue sky. It was turning out to be a relatively hot day for June. The forest in the Little Yoho Valley as they tackled their descent a few hours later gave them some shade, and it was cooling to hike next to the Yoho River and waterfalls.

When they reached the car, Shane smiled at her. She grinned back, and they set off to their new campground. Neither had mentioned Ryan or the bet or anything to do with life back home since lunch. All they'd talked about were the superb views—the glaciers, the perfect alpine lakes, beautiful flower-filled meadows, and some of the most impressive waterfalls they'd ever seen.

After all, while walking through paradise, nothing else really seemed to matter.

Chapter 11

THAT NIGHT, WHILE SHANE secured their tents, Krista sat on a log and finished washing their dinner plates in a bowl of cold water. They'd cooked a simple pasta meal together when they'd got back from their hike, though the drive out here took longer than they'd thought and the sun was already setting by the time they'd parked up. Now, clouds had covered the moon, throwing their backcountry campground—which was really a cluster of clearings linked by narrow trails—into more darkness. It was so quiet here too, and not at all like the night before at Lake Louise, which had been full of families and facilities.

All they had here was a cold-water pump by the campground's entrance and a hut that passed as a washroom.

Krista didn't mind at all about having only the bare basics, but after the sunshine and brightness of the day, it felt a little. . . *spooky* around here.

Which totally meant she should get a grip—and definitely not let on to Shane that she was a wimp in the nighttime wilderness.

Drying the last bowl, she called out to him, "Do you need a hand?"

"No, I'm good, thanks." Like a coal miner, Shane wore a light on his head. The beam flashed through the darkness as he moved. "I'm almost done."

"I'll go put these in the car, then." She left him to it and placed the bowl of clean dishes in the trunk, next to their food supplies, which were placed in clip-closed metal tubs. They weren't taking any chances with bears, and too bad that these mosquitoes that kept buzzing around her face didn't take the hint either. She'd already sprayed a ton of repellent all over herself.

Shutting the trunk, Krista went to sit in the car and started to look through Shane's trail maps, but after a few minutes of being cocooned from the great, dark outdoors, her gaze drifted to the glove box again where her phone was stored. Had Ryan messaged her?

Checking her phone would bring the world she knew back to her, and after such a peaceful day, she had mixed feelings about inviting her normal life into this vacation.

But as she stared at the glove box, common sense screamed at her that she should at least let her mom and Lisa know about the change of plans to her vacation. Anything could happen out here, and no one in her family knew that she was no longer staying at the Banff Spa Resort and had taken off with Shane.

Krista switched on her phone, and the one bar of signal displayed on her screen was just enough to let a few messages bleep through. The first one she saw was from Ryan. Her pulse kicked up, part surprised, part angry and annoyed, part. . . excited? She didn't know how she felt about him anymore. He'd become displaced in her heart and in her life, and she still hadn't figured out where he now belonged.

She read his message.

How's the hiking with Shane? Are you actually *with* him?

So Ryan was curious, but curiosity wasn't jealousy. And still the fact remained that he'd chosen Zoey, so why was Krista even trying to read between the lines of his simple message? And wasn't it interesting that he *still* hadn't mentioned Zoey? Ryan couldn't know that Krista had seen them making out on the hotel bench. So when would he tell her that he and Zoey were now a couple?

Or was Shane right? Was Zoey just a fling? A one-off?

Krista's anger spiked. So much for thinking Ryan was a close friend. He wasn't telling her anything, so she ignored his questions and messaged him back with the single line of truth she could manage.

`Having a great time. See you all at Calgary Airport on Sunday for the flight home.`

"All" meant the rest of their co-workers. She didn't want Ryan to get the impression that he was still the focus of her attention, nor that she was still the same old faithful Krista who'd come running the moment he called. She sent her message then texted Lisa to tell her what had happened and where she was.

Lisa's reply came through immediately.

`Ryan and Zoey!!! You serious?`

`Yes, I saw them together. Kissing. Ryan is now in the past.`

She told Lisa about Shane asking her along on his hiking tour.

`Just the two of you? Well, hello stranger and what have you done with my sister?`

`What do you mean?`

`As if you don't know? Shane McDermit is yummy!`

Okay. Well, sure. Shane didn't have two heads and a wart on the end of his nose, and all right, he was handsome if you liked fair-haired jock types. But Krista didn't. She preferred dark, artistic-looking men, with warm, soft centers and kind, gentle natures. Like her first long-term boyfriend, Eric, and well, also like Ryan—for whatever good that did her.

So you're all alone in the woods? Just you
and Shane? However will you pass the time?

Get your mind out of the gutter. It's not
like that between us.

Oh, please. Why not?

Because we're just friends. That's why.

Then another message pinged in from Lisa.

He can be your rebound guy.

Krista sighed. Lisa always thought men should be used in some way.

No. We're just friends!!!

Okay, if you say so. Have fun in the woods
then! it sounds very Blair Witch Project.

Oh, man. Why did Lisa have to bring up the one film that had kept Krista awake for weeks!? And even the series of laugh out loud emojis Lisa had tagged on to the end of that last messaged didn't smooth out the hairs at the back of Krista's neck. She shivered. That stupid film had haunted her for weeks after she'd been coerced into watching it—and others like it—last Halloween. She'd wanted to watch a sweet and fluffy rom-com, but as usual, she'd gone along with what everyone else, including Ryan, had wanted.

She texted Lisa back.

It's nothing like The Blair Witch Project
here. I'll be in touch in a few days.

Krista then texted her mom, told her where she was, and quickly switched off her phone. She placed it back in the glove box then pressed her face against the car window and peered at the forest surrounding her. Trees stuck out like bones from the ground and loomed dark against the night sky. *What if someone came out from the shadows?* Her pulse picked up. *What if they heard someone screaming in the distance?*

Scenes from the film flashed before her, and her heart hammered in her chest, her imagination running wild.

A knock on the window made her scream.

"Oops. Did I scare you?" Shane chuckled.

Jesus Murphy! Krista blew out a breath and got out of the car, pushing Shane—who was still laughing—aside with the door.

"Hey," he said. "Doesn't this place remind you of those horror films?" He shone his flashlight into the trees. "You know, where a group of teenagers tell ghost stories around a campfire, and then one goes missing and—"

"Stop it. I've just had my sister texting to say the same thing. What is it with you people?"

Shane up lit his face with the flashlight, his eyes wide and zombie-like. "Us dead people?"

"Very funny." She pushed past him. "I'm going to the washroom."

"Toilet."

"Whatever." *What they had out here didn't pass for either, anyway.*

She grabbed her washbag from the trunk then hesitated as she gazed at the path that disappeared into darkness.

"Want me to escort you?"

Yes! But he'd only tease her, and she'd never live it down.

"I'll be fine." Krista swallowed, aimed her flashlight at the path, and headed toward it. Behind her, Shane howled like a werewolf. "Oh, you're just so hilarious!"

"That wasn't me," he called back, sniggering. "Must've been a cougar."

"I hope it eats you first, then!"

Shane's laughter followed her all the way to the washroom hut, and as she peed—in record time—he sang the chorus of "Who's Afraid of the Big Bad Wolf?" By the time she'd cleaned her teeth, he'd moved on to a scary rendition of "Ghostbusters."

So mature.

He was still singing when she got back.

"*The Blair Witch Project* was completely made up, anyway," she told him.

"If you say so." Shane snorted. "Will you be okay here for five minutes while I go and get more water?"

"Of course I will. I'm going to bed."

"Make sure you zip up tight. You wouldn't want any—"

"Good night, Shane." Krista crawled into her tent.

Shane's footsteps crunched toward the pump, and he was still whistling that same stupid song.

Inside the tent, she hugged her knees—and then she smiled.

Shane was a joker. He liked to play games, for sure.

And she knew exactly how to pay him back.

THE PUMP WORKED A treat, even if the water was ice cold. Still smiling, Shane filled up their bottles. He hadn't expected kick-ass Krista to be so jumpy, but then again, with all her talk of sweetness and fluff, there was a lot of softness beneath the bolshy. He'd only continued to tease her because she looked like she was expecting ghosts to jump out of her, and he'd kept talking so that his voice would reassure her in the dark.

Okay, maybe he could've chatted about the weather or about their plans for tomorrow's hike instead of singing and howling, but she would probably have sussed that he was pandering to her anyway, and she probably didn't want him to know that she was feeling a little unsettled out here. They were in the middle of the wilderness after all, with only each other for company. So far, they were getting along. Today's hike had been spectacular, and no doubt about it, Krista was good company.

Shane made his way back to camp.

"Hey," he whispered as he approached her tent. "You okay in there?"

He waited a few seconds, but Krista didn't reply. At least she wasn't too scared to sleep, though like him, she was probably too beat to lie awake for very long. They'd covered a lot of ground today, and he was more than ready to hit the sack himself, too.

Quietly, he unzipped his tent and crawled inside.

"I see dead people."

"Argh!" Shane screamed and shot backward from the uplit face in the corner, his blood roaring in his ears.

"Not so funny now, is it?" Krista said, still holding the torch to light up her face in that demonic way.

"You nearly gave me a heart attack!"

"You crapped yourself," Krista hooted.

"You know what this means now, then?"

"What?"

"I have to kill you." Krista squealed as Shane lunged for her and tickled her sides. She was shrieking and giggling so much that she dropped the torch, sending them both into darkness. "There's no one to save you now," he cackled like an evil villain.

"Serves you right!" she said, flat on her back and gasping for air between her laughter. "Just you wait until I tell everyone at work."

"You wouldn't dare." Shane continued to tickle her, dodging her flaying arms and legs, until she was writhing beneath him and he'd somehow sunk between her thighs.

He stilled.

And so did Krista.

Her legs were spread wide and her soft boobs were squashed beneath his chest. He felt them rise and fall with each of her short and shallow breaths, and her mouth was so close to his that he could smell the mint of her toothpaste. Her fingers wrapped around his biceps. *An invitation?* Shane dipped his head a fraction closer to her lips—then halted. *This was Krista.* She was in love with Ryan, for god's sake, and they were only here, together, because of some stupid payback scheme he'd concocted to save another battering to his ego. Not to. . .

"It's—"

"I'd better—"

"Yeah."

Shane rolled off her, and she scooted away from him.

"So!" Krista said, fumbling in the darkness. "We're even, right? You got me. I got you. And...ta-da! Here's the flashlight. Yay!" She switched it on. "See you tomorrow, scaredy cat."

"Yep. See you tomorrow." Shane angled his body so Krista could shuffle out of his tent. Her leg brushed against his thigh, and a thousand volts shot through him. A flash reminder of how close they'd been just a few seconds ago.

And how it had felt so damn hot.

Chapter 12

An hour into their hike around Emerald Lake the next morning, Krista's trained eye detected something not quite right with Shane's stride.

She'd been walking behind him for the past twenty minutes—looking at his hard butt as much as she'd been looking at their glorious surroundings—so she should know when his gait was giving off little signs of struggle. Shane had also been quieter than usual all morning.

"Your left leg is compensating for something going on in your right hip flexor," she said. "Have you pulled something?"

"It's just some tightness in my thigh," he said. "It'll wear off when my muscles have warmed up."

"I can take a look at it for you later if you want."

"I'll be 'right," he drawled then nodded to the logs and rocks by the lake shore. "Mind if we stop to take some photos of the water?"

"Sure."

Joining Shane on the lakeshore, she pulled her water bottle out of her bag, and out dropped a packet of tissues with it. Shane picked them up and handed them to her.

"Thanks."

The tips of her fingers brushed his, and her stomach zinged—just like it had last night in his tent.

Oh, man. Last night. . .

She hadn't brought up her prank this morning, and neither had Shane.

Just as well, because she didn't want any awkwardness to ruin their day. They'd only been messing around anyway. It meant nothing. To either of them.

If only her body would get the message. Not that she could blame her poor hormones for revving up. Shane was big and solid, and she hadn't had a man on top of her in forever.

But so what if, for a split second, it had felt like he'd been about to kiss her? She of all people knew not to read too much into such things—after all, hadn't she been reading into every tiny signal from Ryan these past few months? And look where that had gotten her.

What happened last night was just a silly joke, taken that little bit too far. Nothing else. Nothing more. So she shook the sexy thoughts out of her mind and turned her attention to something practical and sensible instead.

"I'll cook tonight," she said in true cozy Krista style. "Just let me know what rations are on the menu."

"Actually, I was thinking about a burger and chips at that Moose Head Lodge we passed by earlier. Are you up for that?"

"Too freaking hell I am," she whooped. Her face had been pressed against the window when they'd driven by earlier. "But I'll buy. It's the least I can do."

Shane merely shrugged and gazed at the view as he munched his apple. The sun caught the tips of his blond eyelashes, making them look longer than Krista had ever noticed before, and there was a light stubble on his jaw. Until now, she'd only ever seen him clean shaven, and she had to admit, Lisa was right. He did look *yummy*.

Get a grip, Krista.

She had no right thinking Shane was *yummy* in any respect. They were friends on an impromptu vacation together, and he wasn't interested in her any more than she was interested in him. Unexpected physical contact and the hot, sunny day were making her horny, that was all. Big deal. For someone who hadn't had sex in over a year, it was a natural reaction. A chemical reaction.

And that pesky zing to her stomach last night when he'd lain on top of her?

Completely forgotten.

OR RATHER, IT WAS forgotten—*almost*—until Shane, back at camp later that evening, walked up the path through the trees shirtless and dripping wet after his wash at the pump.

What was it with these zings?

Krista saw shirtless athletes all the time. It was her job to *touch* shirtless athletes all the time. Hard, sculpted pectorals and abdominals were all in a day's work for her.

So, why the electricity zapping through her system, making her want to lick her lips and growl?

"Give me a sec and I'll be ready," he called out.

They were heading out for dinner at the Moose Head Lodge.

Krista wore a T-shirt dress and comfy sneakers. Shane, by the looks of it, would wear shorts and a soft-looking shirt he was currently buttoning up over his pecs, totally oblivious to how his bare chest was making her insides turn to goo.

How would *he* feel if she paraded topless in front of him after her wash at the pump?

Now that was a thought that didn't help one bit to ease the squirmy feeling between her thighs.

Holy smokes, she was a dry desert coming to life after a few drops of rain.

When and how had the landscape become so barren?

AN ENORMOUS PAIR OF antlers decorated the bar of the Moose Head Lodge, and the mouthwatering aromas of garlic and sizzling beef engulfed Shane's senses. He clutched his growling stomach. "Strewth almighty, I could eat a moose."

Beside him, Krista giggled. He liked the sound of it, and her smile, and the way she'd laughed last night when she'd played her joke and he'd tickled her. Too bad that had all got out of hand.

All day, he hadn't been able to shake how she'd felt beneath him out of his mind, how her body had fit so deliciously—so perfect-ly—against his. Strewth almighty indeed. He was hungry for more than just something to eat, and yup, that was just. . . too bad.

Krista only had eyes for Ryan Dubois, and Shane had never been into women who loved other men. Call him selfish, but he preferred his girlfriends to be solely focused on him when they were together, not dreaming about—or shagging—other fellas.

Now, now, McDermit. There you go again, comparing every woman to Fiona.

"Let's see what looks good." Shane reached for a menu at the same time as Krista, and their fingers touched. He pulled his hand back, ignoring the crackles of whatever the hell that was soaring through his system again, like it had by the lake when he'd handed her tissues. Why now was touching Krista like touching a live wire?

"After you," he said, his full-on poker face deployed. "I know what I want already."

"Burger and fries?"

"With all the trimmings."

"Me too."

They ordered at the counter.

"I'll have a Molson too, please," Krista told the woman behind the bar then turned back to Shane. "You wanna share the bottle with me, seeing as you're driving?"

"Sure. I can tolerate a few sips of your mediocre national beer."

The bartender snorted.

"Ignore him," Krista said to her. "He's Australian." Then she grabbed her bottle and pulled Shane away. "I bet you Aussies could learn a thing or two about beer from us Canadians."

"I doubt it, but if you want to lose another bet..."

"I've not lost the first one."

"Yet."

Krista took a sip of Molson and watched him with narrowed eyes. "You still think Ryan will be jealous, eh?"

Shane was sorry to bring that dweeb back into center play, but how else would he stop thinking about how good it had felt lying between Krista's thighs? Reminding himself that she was besotted with Ryan was better than a cold shower.

"Ryan will be at your feet by Sunday," he said firmly, because after last night, he was definitely in need of that cold shower.

"What if I don't want him at my feet?"

"Then I guess you kick him away."

"Like one of those irritating yappy dogs?" Krista let out a little laugh as she shook her head. "But then I'd've lost a hundred bucks for nothing. Maybe I should just give him a big sloppy kiss instead and make my loss worthwhile?"

"Maybe." Shane would rather she kicked him away, but really, it was none of his business. "Let's grab that booth over there by the pool table."

"Do you want a game after we've eaten?" she asked, seeming just as happy as he was to let the subject of Pretty Boy drop. "We could do best out of three."

"Sure, but no hustling. I saw you play the other night, and you were pretty good."

"Ugh. Don't remind me," Krista groaned. Her cheeks turned pink, and Shane's brain filled with that strip of red lace he'd seen that night through the tear in her pants as she'd pressed her backside against his crotch. "I learned a big lesson that night and another one the morning after." She took a seat in the booth, and Shane slid in opposite her, annoyed that the subject was back onto Ryan again. Shaking her head, she added, "Lisa told me to grab the bull by the balls."

"Well, ouch. It's horns, not balls."

"I know, right? That's what I told her! I should've listened to myself, and then. . . well, you know what happened." Krista slumped over the table and sighed. "Should've known better than to try being someone I'm not."

"And who were you trying to be?"

"My sister, I guess. Apart from her experience with Deranged Duane, she's always so carefree and confident with men," Krista sighed. "She has a good time, and then she moves on. She flicks her hair, and more come running. I sometimes wish I could be like that."

"Why?"

"I guess it seems more fun. I dunno." Krista shrugged. "I sometimes feel kinda boring by comparison."

Krista boring? There hadn't been a dull moment since they'd taken off together, but he didn't want to mention it in case it sounded *flirty.*

So he settled for annoying instead and flicked a beer mat at her. "Are you feeling sorry for yourself again?"

"Yeah." But she was smiling up at him, like she knew she was entitled to feel any damn way she wanted to feel. "Got a problem with that?"

"Not particularly." Shane took a sip of her beer and pulled a face. "But if you're gonna drown your sorrows, at least do it with a decent drink."

This time, she flicked the beer mat at him.

He caught it as it slid off his shoulder and grinned. "You're not bad just as you are, Krista Gervais."

"Right back at ya, Shane McDermit."

Chapter 13

SITTING ACROSS THE TABLE from each other, like a couple on a date, Krista watched Shane sprinkle salt on his fries. Never in a million years had she thought they'd get along so well, and that wasn't just her raging hormones talking. Shane really was a breath of fresh Rocky Mountain air—no, a big gust of cliff top wind, swooshing in out of nowhere to blow the cobwebs away and make everything shiny and new and exciting again. She was so glad to have him as a friend.

But then, for the gazillionth time, the position they'd ended up in last night sprang to mind again. Her libido jumped up like an excitable puppy. *Down, girl! You're barking up the wrong tree with Shane.* Yeah, he was a friend now, but he was also clearly one of those guys who didn't do long-term relationships and commitment. The kind of guy she'd never been attracted to.

But maybe, when she got back to Vancouver, Krista could try out the dating scene to find just the kind of guy she'd always wanted. Maybe she'd go out for cocktails with Lisa and get back into the swing of meeting men.

Hmm. Cocktails and nightclubs weren't really Krista's style, but how else did couples meet? She'd already had her college romance with sweet, dependable—*and okay, let's face it, boring*—Eric. And she'd also had a workplace romance that never was with Ryan. . . which had now become a red flag waving never to go down that route again.

Dating a co-worker was risky.

She was already dreading returning to work and coming across Ryan and Zoey, holding hands or canoodling in the gym's café bar area. Awkward. Krista's co-workers must've known about her crush on Ryan, but at least now with Shane's photos and rumors that they'd hooked up, she wouldn't be getting sympathetic looks from everyone. Even more awkward.

"Hey, you're not still feeling sorry for yourself, are you?"

Realizing she'd been quiet for some time, Krista started. "No, no, I was just thinking about work. I wish I could stay out here for another week, or several months."

"Me too."

She picked up a fry and dunked it in ketchup. "So, tell me when you discovered your love for swimming."

"Probably around the time I found front crawl and breaststroke came a lot easier than writing or reading," he said. "That was before anyone realized I was dyslexic."

"How old were you when you were diagnosed?"

"Ten or eleven, I think. I don't really remember. But when I got to high school, things seemed to click in that department. I had all the tools to help me in the classroom. Then, my dad eventually gave me this stern lecture that basically said I couldn't use dyslexia as an excuse not to study and spend all my time in the pool."

"And were you using it as excuse?"

"I was a thirteen-year-old boy." Shane snorted. "I was using everything as an excuse not to study. In the end, I just got on with it. My grades were good enough for uni. I actually enjoyed learning stuff then, but swimming was my true passion."

"Was?"

"Is. Was." Shane shrugged. "I'm not getting any younger. Every day I feel a new crick, a new ache."

"You've pushed your body hard for twenty years," Krista said. The majority of her patients were athletes whose bodies were showing signs of wear and tear from their sport. "Is that why you're retiring?"

"Partly. The love's also gone a bit, if I'm honest."

"Been there, done that, bought the T-shirt?"

"Yeah, something like that." His lips quirked. "What about you? What's your goal?"

"Currently, I'm hoping to travel with Team Canada to the next Olympics. My manager says I have a good shot at it." She nibbled a leaf of salad that had fallen out of her burger. "But ultimately, I'd like my own clinic one day. Working for myself, building a business around family. I dunno. It's so down the line, I haven't really looked into it much yet."

"You will, when the time's right, just like I did."

"You're setting up your own clinic?"

"Not quite. It's sports consultancy and training. I'm planning to lecture at universities back home."

"I bet they'd fall over themselves to have a real Olympian like you working for them."

"Maybe."

"So, tell me what's it like to win gold."

"Amazing."

Krista enjoyed the superhero glint in his eyes. "You must've felt invincible standing on top of the podium."

"It was pretty great, I won't lie," he said then laughed softly. "Until that upstart from Canada came out of nowhere and began to snatch every title from me."

"Ah. The Cocky Canadian," Krista said with a smile. "And you're the Nearly Man. Does that rattle?"

Shane bit into his burger and took his time chewing.

"Gosh, I'm sorry," she added quickly. She'd been so swept up in their conversation, she'd forgotten to be tactful. "You've probably been asked that a million times before. It must be annoying."

"It's okay," Shane said. He took a long sip of his lemonade. "I didn't mind when I lost out to Mikey—he deserved to win every one of those medals—but when the media pounced on the Nearly Man tag after my ex called off our wedding, then yeah, it pissed me off."

Whoa! Brakes screeched in Krista's head.

"You were engaged?"

Holy cow, she hadn't been expecting that! Food lodged in her throat, and she didn't know where to look.

"I've surprised you."

"A little," she coughed.

Love Sucks Shane had once been about to get married?

To whom? And what the hell had happened?

But she couldn't ask such personal questions. Not when they were enjoying a lovely, carefree meal. Not when it wasn't any of her damn business.

"I feel like I've put my foot in something," she said.

"You wear your heart on your sleeve, don't you?" Shane chuckled. The sound surprised her. "Do yourself a favor and never play poker."

"Eh?"

"Never mind. You've not put your foot in anything." Smiling, Shane picked up his burger again. "Once upon a time, I was about to get married. It didn't work out. I moved on. I barely think about it now."

"Still, it must've been very upsetting at the time."

"Meh." Shane shrugged and continued to eat.

Okay. Maybe not that upsetting, then.

One woman was pretty much like another to him. He'd said so himself, and fair enough if that's what he believed. Who was Krista to tell him any different? Holding out for love and romance and a steady, solid relationship hadn't exactly brought her a boatload of happiness lately.

In fact, all it had done was deprive her body of the sex she'd been thinking about all day.

·♥·♥·♥·♥·♥·

BIG FAT LIAR. . .

Of course Shane thought about his abandoned wedding. More so this week than these past few months.

As he drove back to their camp, tomorrow's date flashed before him. His first wedding anniversary.

Or would have been if This Time Last Year had gone to plan.

So, yeah, he was thinking about his wedding, and he was thinking about Fiona too. She was a constant earworm, chanting a song of disappointment and shattered dreams.

The only thing that drowned her out was Krista.

Could he ever love a woman again?

Alright, maybe not love. But fun. Could he have fun times—and yes, damnit—could he have sex with someone and not think about the Bad Times?

Sex with Krista was out of the question—he'd put a lid on that urge last night—but in theory, he could start casually dating when he got back home to Sydney. But that was six months away, and if lying between Krista's thighs last night had driven him to such distraction today, he seriously needed to get laid soon—only *not* with Krista.

Three days ago, she'd been crying over Ryan. That pain on her face couldn't go completely away so quickly. And in what universe could he ever say, *Hey Krista, how's about us having a little no-strings fun?*

Not his universe, that's for sure, and certainly not when they still had three hiking days left together and she was likely to say, *No, Shane, what the hell are you thinking?*

Chapter 14

SHANE PARKED THE CAR next to their tents and cut the engine.

"Let's go and sit on the log over there," Krista said, handing him one of the beers they'd brought back with them from the Moose Head Lodge.

The sun had almost dipped behind the mountains, already turning them a delicate shade of pink. Everything was so quiet and peaceful here, and he couldn't remember the last time he'd felt so quiet and peaceful too.

They sipped their beers, but soon the flaming mozzies ruined the mood. He swotted one away from his face then swiped at one hovering above Krista's head.

"They're out in full force tonight," Shane said as they ducked back into the car to finish their drinks.

Krista sat behind the wheel, insisting he take the passenger side so he had more room for his legs, and they set about making plans for tomorrow's hike to the Edith Cavell glacier. Krista's hair fell around her face as she read the trail guide on her lap.

"It says here to prepare ourselves for some stunning mountain views," she said. "You know what that means?"

"Prepare ourselves for a beast of a climb."

"Correct. No pain, no gain." Krista snickered.

Shane finished his beer. Krista finished hers.

Tucking her legs under her, she cozied up in the driver's seat, seemingly in no rush to get to her tent. Shane stretched out his legs in the footwell, in no rush either.

"The Icefields Parkway bike ride was a fun experience," Krista said. "I wonder how much money you all raised."

"I heard close to two million."

Krista whistled. "That's awesome."

Shane agreed. It had felt good taking part in an event that would ultimately benefit others. Though he wasn't sure if his left thigh would agree. He'd been ignoring the tightness for a few days, but it was becoming clear that he may have pulled something during the race. With the heel of his palm, he kneaded the top of his leg.

"Is your thigh still bothering you?" Krista asked. "Want me to take a look at it for you?"

Have Krista touch him so close to his groin?

He swallowed. "It's okay. You're on holiday, and I—"

"Shane, it really isn't a problem, especially after all you've done for me. I can at least check you over and make sure it's nothing serious that will affect your training next week." Krista pushed her car door open then looked over her shoulder. "Your tent or mine?"

"Mine," Shane almost growled. Just the thought of having Krista in his tent again made him hard, but she was right. If he'd pulled a muscle, it needed to be seen to. As it was, this week off—though much needed—had set his schedule back, and he couldn't afford any more delays in his training, not with the Pan Pacific Championships coming up at the end of the year.

And treatment from Krista wouldn't take long. It wasn't like she'd be giving him an all-over body massage.

Great.

Now he had another image to get out of his head.

"You coming?" she called out.

And another one.

When Shane joined Krista in the tent, she was already on her knees, rubbing what looked like a bar of soap in her hands. It smelled like strawberries. He got in beside her and lay down, the flap of the tent closed and cutting out most of the light.

"I haven't got any massage lotion with me," she said. "You'll have to put up with my moisturizer bar. I hope that's okay?"

"No worries." Shane unzipped his shorts and shimmied out of them.

Stretching out his leg for Krista to examine, he explained in his most professional manner which muscle pinched. When Krista placed her firm fingers on his bare thigh, his voice raised a few octaves. Clearing his throat, he laid back onto his elbows, and while Krista pressed into this thigh, he tried to focus on the construction and material of his tent.

Those fiberglass poles were a true marvel. So light and flexible yet strong. . . and not helping in the slightest to distract him from his current predicament. Memories of Krista's hotness last night as she'd writhed beneath him taunted him. As her fingers worked the tension out of his leg, the tension in his pants increased, gearing his dick up for action that wouldn't—couldn't—happen.

She's in love with Ryan, remember?

"Man, you're hard here," Krista said, working her thumbs down his IT band.

She didn't know the half of it!

Thank god the light had faded and she wouldn't be able to see his boxers pitching.

"I need to rig up a light to see you better," she said.

"No, it's okay. You've done more than enough, thank you." Shane shifted—at the same time that Krista reached over for his head torch.

She toppled against him then froze.

And Shane didn't need a light to see the shock on her face.

·♥·♥·♥·♥·♥·

The semidarkness hadn't been playing tricks on her after all!

Pressed against Shane's erection, Krista knew she hadn't mistaken that swell in his boxer shorts.

Freaking hell!

When was the last time she'd turned a man on like this? All those times she'd cozied up on the couch with Ryan, not once had he shown any desire toward her. Not even when they'd kissed.

But Shane?

Holy smokes.

As someone who touched other people's bodies for a living, Krista could instantly tell when one was tense. Shane had been on high alert as soon as he'd gotten into the tent, but her professionalism had kicked in and she'd done her best to ease the awkwardness. After all, she was doing her job. One friend to another.

Until now.

"Krista? Um. . . this isn't what you might think."

"Oh? You're not turned on?"

"Fuck, yeah, but it doesn't mean anything."

"It's just a chemical reaction, right?" She shifted slightly—not off him, just. . . *along* him. It made his breath hitch. "Are you sure it doesn't mean anything?"

"All right, I guess it's pretty obvious what it means," he said, his voice strained, "but it's not like I want anything to happen."

Seriously? Well, wasn't that just the story of her life. Would she ever drive a man to sexual distraction? Couldn't she even make a man like Shane—a man not into love and commitment—lose control with desire?

"I've never had a one-night stand," she said, still lying on him, getting wetter and wetter as his hardness pressed against her, just *there*. "I've never had casual sex."

"I thought as much." Shane's breathing was ragged, like he was pushing weights. "That's why I said it doesn't mean anything. So. . . um. . . Krista?"

"Hmm?"

"I'm gonna lie here and count to ten. If you don't want anything to happen between us tonight, you leave. Okay?"

A shot of arousal revved her system up another thousand notches. He *did* want to have sex with her!

"One," Shane said.

Eh? "You're seriously counting?"

"Two."

"What about—"

"Three."

Krista burst out laughing. This was ridiculous. For sure, she could leave and they both knew it. There was no need to count. "Shane, I—"

"Four."

"Will you listen—"

"Five."

"C'mon, can you—"

"Six."

Krista grabbed his face and kissed him. His lips were hot, foreign, and delightful, with just the right amount of stubble to make all those zings shoot through her body full force. Deepening the kiss, she swept her tongue against his, her fingers in his hair, losing herself in an assault of thrills and jolts she'd never felt before. When they came apart, they were both panting.

"Ten." Shane placed his hands gently on her hips. "You're still here."

"I am." She rocked against him. "You were counting during the kiss?"

"Of course. I had to make sure."

Krista kissed him again. For one, she wanted to tell him she *was* sure. For two, it turned out Shane was very, very kissable. "Have I sealed the deal?"

"What about Ry—"

"*Shhh*. I don't want to talk about him." Krista laid her hand over Shane's mouth. "In fact, I don't want to talk at all. This is what I want." She rubbed herself against his hard ridge.

The darkness surrounding them, thick with heat and desire, stripped away her self-consciousness and empowered her in the most delicious way. She kissed Shane's forehead, his nose, and then his lips. She was twenty-seven years old. She'd never slept with a guy she hadn't been dating for months. Casual sex was Mom's and Lisa's way.

But tonight, for one night only, it would be her way too.

"Vacations are all about doing stuff you wouldn't normally do, right?" she said.

"Like ice cream for breakfast and cocktails by the pool?"

"Exactly. One night of sex can be our vacation treat." She pressed little kisses at the corner of his mouth, enjoying how hard and taut he'd become beneath her, as if any movement would pop this fragile, yet intense, sexy bubble they'd created. "Do you have condoms?"

"Yes."

Condoms he'd hoped to use with Zoey. But what the hell. Krista had her own stash at the bottom of her bag that she'd hoped to use with Ryan. And what was going on between her thighs right now definitely had nothing to do with Ryan. Or Zoey.

Just Shane.

And how much Krista wanted him to touch her in all her needy, yearning places.

Shane reached and fumbled above his head then pulled out what must be, from the sound of it, a box of condoms from his washbag. He tore it open. She couldn't see the expression on his face, but she could tell by his jagged breathing that his jaw would be set firmly and that his body was already primed and ready for action beneath hers.

He wants me.

So, why wasn't he in a hurry to put the condom on?

What was he waiting for?

When he pressed the foil packet into her palm, Krista understood. He wanted the final decision to be with her. She smiled in the darkness. She'd never been this turned on. Never felt this powerful.

Running her fingers over the hard contours of his groin and lower abs, she took her time feeling her way around his body, causing him to hiss and hold his breath, before rolling the latex to his hilt. He pulsed against her fingers, and when Krista could no longer bear the ache between her legs, she mounted him.

His soft, guttural groans mixed with hers, filling the night air. Shane was thick and hard inside her—so exquisite—and when he gripped her butt and jacked his hips, Krista let herself go, wanting nothing more than to ride this magnificent man into the night.

Chapter 15

Birds crowing in the trees woke Krista with a start early the next morning. Plastered against Shane's broad—*bare*—back, she hazily recalled that at some point in the night, between lovemaking sessions, he'd retrieved her mattress and sleeping bag from her tent, and they'd fallen asleep crammed against each other.

Which wasn't a bad thing, just. . . unusual.

It being her first one-night stand, Krista didn't know quite know what to do or how to behave. Quietly, she peeled herself away from Shane's hot skin. Cool air slicked her bare breasts, bringing her attention to the alarming fact that she was butt naked. *Jesus Murphy, what had she done?* She fumbled quietly for her clothes and dressed in a hurry.

Last night had been dirty, sexy, and wonderful, and she'd been so brazen and bold!

But she hadn't given a thought to how it would be between them in the harsh light of The Morning After. Seduced by the earthy wilderness, they'd gotten carried away—*she'd* gotten carried away. Her cheeks were already burning with the awkwardness that would no doubt hang around her and Shane for the next few days, pretending nothing ever happened. Because really, hiking together afterwards wasn't how one-night stands were meant to go, was it? Weren't they all about making a hasty getaway after a perky, *Thanks, that was fun* and a quick, *See you around*?

Just like Lisa's conquests did. Krista would often hear them at dawn, trying to figure out how to open the locks on the front door. But she couldn't exactly slip out into the street and hail a cab home out here. So, what were the next three days going to be like?

Cursing her lack of foresight, Krista slowly creaked the tent's zipper up high enough for her to crawl out.

A warm hand wrapped around her calf and stopped her.

"Did you leave the money on the side for me, baby?" Shane drawled.

"Very funny." She eased his hand off her leg.

"You gonna run away and hide from what happened last night, Krista, or are you gonna own it?"

Now, what did that mean?

"I don't run away and hide from anything," she said, and to prove it, she looked him straight in the eye—until he sat up and the sleeping bag dropped low past his hips. Krista's gaze shifted to his chest and down his abs. Last night in the dark, she'd licked his nipples and fondled every part of his naked body. Her mouth went dry at the memory. Her brain scrambled. She said the first thing that came to mind. "I really need to pee."

"Go ahead and relieve yourself, my mistress." Shane lay back down with a regal wave of his hand. "I'll be here for when you require my services again."

"Thanks, but it was a *one*-night stand, remember?" She scurried out and ran to the washroom. She'd meant what she'd said last night. She and Shane would only have one night of sex, because doing it again—and again—would mean they'd started a *thing*.

And Krista didn't do *things*.

She did solid, long-lasting relationships, based on friendship and understanding. And she couldn't—wouldn't—waste her time and energy on yet another man who didn't want the same things she did.

So, just one wild night it would remain. A summer vacation treat that they'd both needed.

And man, had she needed it.

A giggle bubbled up inside her. She really had been so demanding last night! She'd thoroughly used Shane for her sexual pleasure, telling him exactly what she liked and how she liked it—which he must've gotten a lot out of too, if his hot, hard need for her body had been anything to go by.

She was still smiling when she returned to camp.

Until the sight of a shirtless Shane wiped it clean off her face. He was boiling water for coffee, and when he saw her, he merely raised one eyebrow as if to say, *You looking at me?*

Too right, she was.

Elite athletes like Shane McDermit trained super-humanly hard. Those sculpted pecs, shoulders, and biceps—those molded abs... They took years of discipline and commitment to develop. A body like his *should* be looked at. It should be appreciated.

And Shane's slow smile told her he liked her appreciation. Very much.

Krista stopped drooling and cleared her throat. "So, um. . . did you sleep okay?"

"Eventually." Shane's lips quirked as he handed her a cup of coffee. He then lifted his own to his lips, keeping his gaze steady on hers.

"We agreed one night only," she said, shooting down that look in his eyes. "The vacation treat, remember?"

"I didn't say anything." Shane merely shrugged, like all he'd been doing was polishing his halo.

Huh.

"I'll pack up while you get ready." Krista ducked inside her tent to prepare for the day's hike, grateful to be away from Shane's loaded gaze for a few minutes. She needed to get her head together, but man, just the thought of how ramped up and turned on she'd been last night was making her damp between her thighs and hot around her neck.

Talk about losing all inhibition!

Where had all this inner primal lust come from?

And why hadn't it ever come to the surface before?

·♥·♥·♥·♥·♥·

A COUPLE OF HOURS later, as they hiked a trail near their camp that promised views of the Edith Cavell glacier, that question still bounced around Krista's head.

Why had Shane turned her on so much?

For sure, he had an impressive body and he was fun to be with, but they were friends, and she'd never pounced on a friend like that before.

It must have been the two Molsons she'd drunk and the cover of darkness, giving her extra confidence to have her vacation treat and eat it too, as well as the obvious—hard—fact that Shane had wanted *her*.

This was his fault. The lovely meal they'd shared. The moonlight and the wilderness afterwards. It had given him ideas of romance.

Well, no, not romance.

Just wanton, unadulterated sex.

And of course, sex and love were entirely different things. Which was another reason she shouldn't read anything into last night.

Casual sex was just casual sex! She'd be wise to repeat that mantra to herself every time Shane popped into her mind.

"Do you want to try out this side trail?" Shane asked, looking up from his map. He nodded toward a seemingly lesser-trodden track through the trees. "It says in the guide that it leads to a rocky view of the Athabasca River."

"Sure, sounds awesome." Krista followed Shane down the narrow track.

"The ground here is so mossy. I can just about make out the trail. It's overgrown."

They were back to the business of hiking. Back to talking about the terrain and the beautiful scenery. Shane had stopped looking at her in that way that said *Last night, eh?* and was his usual focused and disciplined self. A good thing. A really good thing. Because Shane thought love was for losers, and getting involved with a man who thought such a thing wasn't in Krista's DNA.

Bushes covered the trail. Shane stepped over a decomposing log that had weeds growing out of the cracks in the rotting bark.

"Are you sure we're still on the right track?"

"Yeah. Doesn't look like anyone's been here in a while, but I can hear the river."

And sure enough, the sound of rushing water got louder and louder. Ten minutes later, the trees cleared a little and they came to a rocky bank that, just as the trail guide had promised, gave them a clear, wide view of the river. Some parts flowed quickly. Others were still and smooth, reflecting clouds and the surrounding forest.

Krista took in the tall wide spruces across the water and the forever-present mountain peaks. "It's so pretty here."

Shane's gaze heated the side of her face. Slowly, she turned to him. Avoiding eye contact with him had been easy on the narrow trail, but now, there was nowhere to hide.

"I want to see you naked," he said. "I want to see every inch of your body. I want to see your face when you come."

Krista's breath hitched, her cheeks on fire. "You. . . um. . . What did you say?"

"You heard."

Her legs weakened. She leaned against a tree.

It was a mistake.

In an instant, Shane stood before her. She had enough space to get around him if she wanted to, but her feet stayed rooted to the ground. God, he looked so hot staring down at her like that. Such desire in his eyes—solely directed at her. She didn't want to walk away.

"So much for just one night, eh?" she said.

"I never actually agreed to that part."

No, he hadn't, and she'd obviously been kidding herself too.

"It's an hour's walk back to camp," she said. Which was plenty of time for this Rocky Mountain heat between them to cool off.

"I was a Scout, remember?" Shane tapped his pocket. "I came prepared."

"What? You want to do it out here! In the open? But anyone can walk by."

"We haven't seen another person since we left the Moose Head yesterday."

Krista looked around her, as if she were expecting to see throngs of people to prove him wrong, but there were only trees and boulders, and they were quite secluded from the main trail. "What about the bears?"

"We'll keep the noise down so they don't get curious. And believe me, I'm so hard for you right now, it won't be an endurance race."

Krista's gaze dipped to the impressive bulge in Shane's shorts.

But, but. . .

Oh to hell with it.

She licked her lips. "What are you waiting for, McDermit?"

At that, his mouth was on hers. Hot and sweet and greedy, easing off only to fumble with the zipper of her shorts. His fingers tugged and pulled and yanked, frustration lacing every groan as he continued to kiss her.

"Next time we go hiking, wear a dress," he growled.

"Got it."

"And no underwear. Underwear is strictly forbidden."

"Whatever you say." She eventually slipped off her shorts and panties, and Shane slipped on a condom. With his shorts halfway down his hips, he stood to attention between the zipper. She parted her legs, wanting him so damn bad—which just went to prove how feral she'd gone in this wilderness! And Shane? He was her own private mountain man, on hand to see to her needs. "Get inside me now."

He thrust into her, and *damn*—he felt so freaking amazing. She groaned out, and when he pushed deeper, Krista wrapped her legs around his waist and tugged his mouth down to hers again. He lifted her up, his large hands cupping her bare butt, squeezing her tight against him.

"I never knew you were this hot, Krista."

Well, neither did she!

"So hot," Shane gasped as he pumped harder and faster. Like hers, his breathing was heavy, but he held on to her as if she weighed nothing. Sensations gathered heat and pace inside her, building and building and—

"Oh, Shane!" Krista came hard, and a split second later, Shane ground out his release as he held her in his arms.

Birdsong mixed with the sound of trees swaying in the breeze and the river gushing below. When Krista finally raised her head off Shane's chest, he was gazing down at her, looking as stunned and dazed as she felt by the intensity of what had just happened between them.

And they still hadn't seen each other naked.

Chapter 16

Al fresco sex in bear country wasn't the smartest idea Shane ever had, but with last night still consuming his body and soul, how could he have resisted Krista today?

This morning, she'd been all shy and ridiculously embarrassed—for what? For being hot and sexy and just so damn alluring?

Where had this attraction come from? He'd seen her dozens of times at the sports center—and even last night when she'd been all dressed up at the hotel. Not once had his radar bleeped. Not even when her pants had ripped and she'd had her butt in his groin in a position that was now getting him all hot and bothered just thinking about taking her that way.

Put simply, he couldn't get enough of her.

And that look on her face this morning when she'd tried to sneak out of his tent, how she'd nibbled her lip and crinkled her brow. What had been going through her mind? Doubts and more doubts, shame and guilt? Well, he hadn't wanted that. Not when they'd had so much fun—and definitely not when it reminded him so much of himself during The Bad Times.

Back then, when he'd come to his senses, doubts, shame, and guilt had been top of his list of emotions to work through, and he'd hated that Krista might feel that way too about what they'd done. He'd also hated her dismissing last night as a one-night stand. No way would he add her to that sordid category. She was too unique, too special. For one, he knew her name. For another, he couldn't spend the rest of this holiday walking next to her—or lying in tent a few meters away—and not touch her again.

So why not have a holiday affair and keep this fire burning for a few more days? Krista had said it herself. . . Sex between them was a vacation treat. And if the demands she'd made of him last night were anything to go by, Shane had suspected she'd want more too.

He hadn't been wrong.

Against the tree, she'd been as ready to explode as much as he was, and now they were hightailing it back to camp, having aborted their hike in favor of more sex in his tent. Not that either of them had actually said that out loud.

It was time for some clarity. Shane snatched up Krista's hand and drew her to him. When she slammed against his chest, he kissed her startled mouth, giving her a clear image of exactly what he wanted when they got back to camp. Her lips instantly softened against his, and when she slipped her tongue into his mouth, he deepened the kiss until her hot body melted against his.

"Where did that come from?" she asked when they eased apart. Her lips were red, her cheeks flushed, and her chest rose and fell as she controlled her breathing.

Shane smiled, liking the effect he was having on her. Arousal was a good look on Krista.

"We have today, tomorrow, and Saturday," he said. "Three days, three nights, plus Sunday morning. We'll still do plenty of hiking, but there are plenty of other things to do too. So. . ."

"So. . ?" For a long moment, her serious gaze flickered all over his face, like she was searching for an answer to his unspoken proposal.

Shane held his breath, and then her hands were on either side of his face, pulling him down for a hungry, desperate kiss that screamed *Hell yeah!*

Grabbing her butt, he yanked her against his still-unsated body, impatient for what would come next. But she slipped out of his arms so quick, she left him pouting.

"Hey!"

"Race you back!" she called out and darted down the trail.

Shane snapped out of his heated daze. She'd shed her backpack at his feet, quicker without the extra weight. "Sneaky!"

He scooped up her bag and ran after her, but he was enjoying the chase too much to overtake. Keeping pace behind her, he sometimes sped up enough to touch her, making out to grab her just for the thrill of hearing her squeal as she darted out of his reach every time. He growled, aroused and mesmerized by the free movement of her sporty body as she ran through the forest.

When they were almost back at camp, Krista darted to the left—toward the water pump.

Breathless, she said, "I need to cool off! I'm all sweaty."

When he caught up with her, she was hanging her head between her knees, gasping for air. Her face was red, and beads of sweat had gathered around her forehead, sticking strands of hair to her skin. A hot, sexy mess.

"You're quick," he said, catching his breath. He dumped her bag on the ground then pushed the pump down so she could drink with both hands and splash her face with cold water. He did the same then gazed down at her. "Don't cool off too much. I haven't finished with you yet."

She choked out a laugh. "I thought cavemen were extinct." But as she stretched out her legs, her gaze dipped up and down his body, like she was already stripping him naked.

He returned the look—because he really did want to strip her naked—and reached out his hand for her.

"Best way to cool off is to take your clothes off," he suggested. "It's a scientific fact."

"I can't argue with science." She slipped her fingers into his, and then she screamed with laughter as he picked her up and threw her over his shoulder. "You really are a caveman!"

She had a point, so he grunted and snatched up her bag with his free hand then carried her back to his tent.

·♥·♥·♥·♥·♥·

OH, MY! SHE'D DIED and gone to heaven.

That was the only explanation for this free and flowing sensation heating her up inside and out. Weightless and untethered.

Shane raised his head from between her thighs and came to lie on top of her. "You liked that?"

"Very much. Couldn't you tell?"

Chuckling softly, he kissed her between her breasts, and she enjoyed the way his appreciative gaze lingered on them afterwards. In fact, Krista was enjoying everything about Shane. His hands on her body, his mouth. The solid thrust of his hips, his broad shoulders. The mound of his thick biceps next to her face as he lay on top of her. Cocooned by his body, she could feel his strength. He was built for power and speed, and yet he was surprisingly gentle and often maddeningly slow—like a few minutes ago, when she'd been desperate for release and he'd continued to tease her with his tongue.

Though it served her right. She'd teased him plenty when they'd first gotten back to the tent. Shane had shed his clothes immediately, but she'd taken her sweet time undressing. It had been fun to watch the anticipation in his eyes, how he'd struggled to steady his breathing. This big, super-fit, super-strong Olympian, undone by her?

She'd *never* had that effect on Eric—or any other guy she'd dated—and definitely not Ryan. But Shane had literally carried her to his bed, wanting her again.

Was he like this with every woman?

And was every woman like this with him?

One woman is the same as any other...

Did he still think that? About her, too?

And what about the woman he'd almost married? Whoever she was must've been special to him. Or maybe not. Yesterday, when he'd mentioned his wedding had been called off, he'd seemed more annoyed about being called a Nearly Man than anything else.

"What's up?" he asked. "You're quiet."

"I was just think—"

"No thinking." He pressed his finger to her lips. "We're on holiday. Ice cream for breakfast, remember?"

"You're right." *Don't ruin it with talk of ex-girlfriends, Krista. This is the hottest sex you've ever had, and you've got it for three more days.* "So, speaking of breakfast, that was a long time ago now. You hungry?"

"Starving." Shane fumbled for his wristwatch, which he'd discarded at some point during their lovemaking, and read out the time. "It's two o'clock. We forgot to have lunch."

"Time flies when you're having fun, eh?"

He leaned over and kissed her. "You are having fun, aren't you?"

"Absolutely." She kissed him back, swiping away all thoughts of his past women and her measly number of past men.

For the next three days at least, there were only two people in this *thing* they'd started. A *thing* she wasn't going to try to figure out. Doing so felt too much like hard work, and keeping ahold of this floaty feeling she got after every orgasm with Shane was much more preferable. Lifting and raising her out of her normal life, this sexual trance was intoxicating. Addictive. And the weirdest thing? Now she could understand Mom's and Lisa's view of casual relationships. Not thinking about Happy Ever After and just enjoying the moment was a lot of fun.

And fun was exactly what she'd promised to have on this vacation.

"Let's eat," she said. "You cook. You're better at it than me."

"Demanding woman." Shane pulled on his pants. "I'll make something quick, and then let's head out to those hot springs for a shower and a soak in the pool. There's a restaurant nearby too. We can have dinner afterwards. I looked up the menu the other day, and they serve Portobello mushroom burgers."

"Giddy up!" Krista fumbled for her clothes. "This is turning out to be the best vacation ever."

He grinned. "Because of the mushroom burgers?"

"Of course. What else?" She kept a straight face, which wiped the smug grin off his.

"What else, huh?" He ran his gaze over her still naked body. "How about the side order of hot sex we're having?"

"Yeah, that ain't bad either." She reached out and squeezed his butt, showing him he was more than a side order. He was very much the main course.

And she wanted many more helpings.

Chapter 17

THE DRIVE OUT TO Miette Hot Springs in Jasper took them back up the Icefields Parkway. As Shane cruised along the same stretch of road he'd biked down the other day, he couldn't help but wonder about the little tricks and spins life sometimes dished out.

Three days ago, riding on a razor-sharp seat alongside Mikey and dozens of other athletes, Shane hadn't even expected to talk to Krista Gervais, let alone get into bed with her. And now she'd ignited this craving inside him, and all he could think about was to keep getting into bed with her, to kiss her and hold her and play with her delightful body. Would he get it—her—out of system by Sunday morning?

"I am desperate for a hot shower," Krista drawled beside him. "I feel so dirty."

"I like my women filthy," he said, making her roll her eyes at him. She knew he was full of shit about most things, but could she see though the player image he'd created for himself? Casual hookups had never been his thing. He'd only started that whole *Hey look at me and how perfect my life is* crap on social media to show his friends and family he was back to being good ol' Shane. He should really drop it now because he'd been his old self for a while—albeit a more cautious, bitter version—but he was doing okay.

His new life plan made sure of it.

But how did Krista fit in with that?

Earlier, he'd stopped Krista from thinking—from asking the questions he didn't, as yet, have answers to. Questions that would burst this steamy little bubble they were currently floating away in. Maybe he should listen to his own words and stop thinking too.

"Well, here we are," he said, clocking the first sign to the hot springs. A few minutes later, he parked the car then took off his wristwatch.

"You stripping already?" Krista asked, a naughty glint in her eye.

Shane grinned, already looking forward to the next time he'd get naked with Krista, but as he opened the glove box, two phones—his and Krista's—stared back at him like two daring eyes. *Pick me up. Switch me on. Check me.*

He snapped the lid shut. "You all good to go?"

"Sure am." Krista was quick to get out.

Shane hadn't seen her check her phone for a couple of days. She hadn't asked about his social media, and neither had mentioned the bet since the Iceline Trail.

That day seemed months ago now. It had been an action-packed—and very satisfying—48 hours. So much had happened.

"I'll hold your hand in the deep end," Krista was saying as they made their way to the entrance. "Or we could see about renting floaties for you while you learn to swim."

"Thanks," he drawled. "If I drown, will you give me mouth to mouth?"

She looked him up and down. "Maybe later," she said when her eyes focused on the *down* part.

Shane laughed, pleased that Krista was no longer *thinking* and was looking forward to *later* as much as he was.

And why not?

They were two healthy adults, planning to spend the next three days together hiking through more stunning scenery and having hot sex in between.

There really was no need to spoil such a pleasant agenda by *thinking*—and Krista's grip on his backside earlier shouted loud and clear that she felt the same way.

As they paid their entrance fee and rented their swimwear—and no *floaties*—Shane couldn't help but snigger to himself at how unashamedly demanding Krista could be when she was turned on.

Sweet and fluffy, my arse.

Krista Gervais liked it hot and spicy and full of thrills.

And from now until Sunday, who was he to deny her of more?

FLOATING IN THE BATH-LIKE water, surrounded by the ever-present mountains, glaciers, and spruces, Krista decide the thermal pools were a gift from the gods. For two hours, she'd bobbed and floated alongside Shane as clouds drifted lazily past above them, not remembering the last time she felt so carefree and relaxed.

They stayed in the water for almost two hours, laughing and chatting sometimes, or quietly floating and not saying much at all. Amazing sex aside, that's what Krista liked best about Shane. He was easy company, and for all of his goofing around and hogwash, what she saw of him was what she got. No brass and bravado, no pretentions or shamming. No games.

And now, as the restaurant buzzed with the chink and clatter of early evening diners, he was making her laugh so much she was getting indigestion.

"You're making that up!" she said, almost choking on her portobello mushroom burger.

"I wish I was! But honest to god, some wanker on Team GB changed the sign on the showers, and the next thing I know, I have all of Team Japan's top female synchronized swimmers gawping at me."

"And you were all soaped up?"

"Like a cream puff." Grinning, Shane popped an olive from his salad into his mouth. "I still don't know what they put in my bar of soap."

Krista hooted again. "And here I thought the Olympics was a serious contest."

"*Pffft.* What made you think that?"

"Only the years and years of dedicated training." Krista dipped a piece of lettuce in mayo. "I guess you'll be training hard for the Pan Pacifics when you get back home."

"They're in December. They'll be over by then."

"Eh? Oh, I meant back home in Vancouver. Next week." But of course Shane called Australia home. "Are you returning to Sydney as soon as they're over, then?"

"Pretty much. I told my parents I'd be home for Christmas this year, and I start training for the Olympics with my old coach in January."

"We'll miss you at the center," she said. *I'll* miss you. Hell, she was even going to miss him on Sunday night when she returned to *her* home—Downtown Vancouver—where she was born and raised. But this wasn't something she'd address right now. *No thinking. Just fun, remember?* She sipped her sparkling water. "So why'd you choose to come to Canada in the first place?"

Shane's smile faltered, and he gave a little shrug. "Stuff happened."

"Like what?"

Slowly, he wiped his mouth with his napkin, and Krista had that same sinking feeling she'd had last night, when he'd told her his ex had called off their wedding.

"I'm sorry. Don't answer that," she said quickly, fearing she'd put her foot in something again.

But was that really the case? Shane didn't do love and romance and serious relationships. . . did he?

Shane took a big bite of his burger, but Krista could only nibble on another piece of lettuce. What had she been like, this woman who Shane had almost married? How long had they been together?

And what had gone wrong?

"Yesterday, you said your wedding had been called off," she ventured. "How long ago was that?"

"Last summer."

"So that's when you decided to transfer your studies to UBC?"

"Yes."

But hold up—if Shane hadn't been bothered by his failed engagement, why move countries? She stared at her plate, the food on it not tasting as good as it did a few minutes ago.

"You wanna know what happened, don't you?" he asked.

"Yeah. I'm curious." Krista shrugged. "But only if you want to share."

"Not really, but here goes." Shane leaned back, and a hardness she'd not seen since that morning in Banff clouded his eyes. "Fiona and I had been together for eight years when I proposed."

Eight years!

But that was most of his adult life!

"I knew she'd say yes," he continued, "because we'd talked about getting married a few times before. We always knew it would be on the cards. We had that kind of relationship."

A random dart of jealousy speared Krista's heart. Love Sucks Shane had been part of a solid, steady couple—*a We*—for almost a decade?

Suddenly, he became a stranger again. And the fact that she barely even liked him three days ago taunted her, poking her off balance. *You may know his body, but you still don't know him.*

"We announced our engagement and had a big party," Shane said, sarcasm dripping off his words. "Everyone was just so delighted for the very happy couple."

"You weren't happy?" Krista asked. Maybe their relationship hadn't been working for him? Maybe he'd changed his mind and he'd no longer wanted to be with this Fiona?

"I was extremely happy. Life couldn't have been better."

Oh.

"I was in love with a woman who loved me back. What more could I ever want?"

But his tone was bitter, and her heart panged at the hurt and vulnerability in his eyes. "So what went wrong?"

"She had an affair. Actually, no. 'Affair' isn't the right word, and neither is cheating. Because both imply a quick fling, a casual hookup. And there'd been nothing casual about her relationship with this other guy."

"How long had she been seeing him?"

"Two years."

Krista choked. "And you had no idea?"

"Nope."

"But it was *two* years. How can you live with someone for that long and not—" The steel in his eyes stopped her. "Gosh, I'm sorry. I shouldn't have said that." Surprise had caused her to be insensitive. There was no point questioning what he did or didn't know, especially when the firm set of his jaw told her he must've questioned it a billion times himself. "I just can't comprehend how someone could have the gall or conscience to lead a double life like that, leaving you to suspect nothing."

"Everyone asked the same question. Our friends couldn't believe it either, but then one by one, they told me they'd had their suspicions."

"And they didn't tell you?"

He shook his head. "They didn't want to upset me, and really, how do you tell someone that you think the woman they're about to marry is seeing someone else?"

"So, what happened next?"

"When she didn't show up, I eventually left the church through a back exit with my best man. And my sister, well, she..." Shane rubbed his face and sighed. "So, the thing about my sister is that she's not the most even-tempered person in the world. She's got three kids, runs on next to no sleep, and has a stressful job in a hospital. . ."

"Oh, god, what did she do?"

"She made the announcement, telling everyone the wedding had been called off. Then outside the church, she bloody ripped through Fiona's family, as in '*You've raised a selfish bitch*' kind of verbal shredding. When I found out, I'd never loved her more, but strewth, she made it all worse. People passing by saw this wedding from hell, where half the guests were having this slinging match, dressed in their finest gear and one step away from a bar brawl. The press got hold of it, and *boom!* It all blew up."

Krista didn't know what to say, so she kept quiet, reading Shane's pain in every crinkle of his brow.

"Gossip sites made me look a fool," he said. "*Fiona* had made me look a fool, because like you said, how could I not have known? And the worst thing? I still damn well bloody loved her. I still wanted her back. I still believed that we could work things out."

Pow! Another bolt of jealousy kicked her when she was already down. *All women are the same* Shane had been in love! Truly, madly, deeply in love.

Why did Krista feel like she'd been lied to?

Why this sense of betrayal?

Folding her arms, she kept all the confusing feelings in check because this wasn't about her. And Shane hadn't lied to her. He was entitled to a private life. A history. She'd just built a different picture of him in her head, and now that picture was turned upside down and inside out.

Managing to keep her voice even, she said, "I guess it's only natural to want the woman you love back."

"It's stupid. *I* was stupid." Shane shook his head, balling the napkin in his fists. "It turned out the other guy knew all about me. He knew about the wedding. He knew she wouldn't leave me."

"And he kept seeing her?"

"Right until the day she finally made up her fucking mind and chose him over me. Two hours before we were due to get married."

"That's awful."

"It's over is what it is. What I said last night was true. I've moved on."

But it didn't take being a physical therapist to see the tension that had built around his neck and shoulders. Or how his good-natured eyes had turned serious and dark. *Poor Shane.* Her heart twanged for the fun-loving guy she'd gotten to know these past few days. How anyone could cheat on someone as hot, nice, and gentle as him was beyond her. But at least now his quick recovery over Zoey and saving face in front of her all made sense. Krista reached out to him.

But he pulled his hand away.

Right. Disappointment shot through her. He didn't want her comfort.

He just wanted her sex.

Chapter 18

HATING HOW THEIR LOVELY day had now turned awkward, Shane leaned over the table and kissed Krista on her lips.

Not a hot, lingering kiss like they'd shared many times before, but a friendly, *Hey, I'm still the same guy you floated in the pool with earlier* kiss that would hopefully get them back on track to enjoying the rest of the evening—and their holiday.

"We still have four hours left of daylight," he said, stepping over the baggage he'd just unloaded between them. *Well, she was the curious one, wasn't she?* It wasn't his fault if she somehow didn't like what she'd just heard. "How about we head out to Medicine Lake? I read it's a great place to see the sunset, and we've got a good, clear sky today. Just the right amount of clouds."

"Yeah, sure. Sounds awesome."

But on the drive out to the lake, the ghost of girlfriends past still lingered between them, making the car feel crowded and claustrophobic.

Krista was quiet.

Shane tapped his fingers on the steering wheel. "Are you okay?"

"Yes, I'm fine."

Fine? He almost laughed. She was pissed off and irritated—*by what?* That he'd had a whole life she didn't know about before he'd slept with her?

He pulled over by the lake and cut the engine.

"Spit it out, Krista."

She folded her arms. "I feel like I don't know you."

"Well, you don't."

"Thanks, asshole." She pushed the door open and stalked out.

Shane drummed the steering wheel then did the same.

"What do you want from me, Krista? My life story? My credit card details? What I got for English in my HSE grades? You tell me yours, and I'll tell you mine."

"Now you're just being a dick."

Yeah, he was. Because the dark, heavy cloud of his damn wedding had loomed over yet another day of his life and pissed all over it. And he was confused and annoyed about Krista's reaction—more so because he damn well *did* understand what she meant about not knowing him, and he was being an arse pretending that he didn't.

Revealing what had happened on his circus show wedding had revealed other things about him, too. All his trash talk about love that first morning in Banff and how, at the Moose Head Lodge, he'd shrugged off the whole debacle like it had meant nothing. He'd led Krista to believe he was a player, a happy-go-lucky guy who never got serious about a woman.

And now she knew differently.

With her back to him, Krista held herself stiffly as she faced the mountains on the other side of the lake.

Treading carefully, he came to stand behind her. Slowly, gently, he placed his hands on her hips. When she didn't shrug him off, he eased her toward him. "By now, you must've figured out why I said all that love is for losers stuff the other day."

"Yeah. Once bitten, twice shy. I can see you're hurt."

"Was. I *was* hurt." Irritation flickered through him. "I am so bloody tired of telling people I've moved on. I've got an excellent life. I don't want people's pity. Or sympathy. I don't want anyone to think I still love Fiona, because I don't."

Krista lowered her head, looking at the ground to where the crystal water gently lapped the stoney shore. Her hair fell to one side, exposing the soft skin of her neck. Could he kiss her there? Would that make it all better between them?

Her jaw tightened. "I didn't like you pulling away from me. I guess I'm not used to people doing that when I'm offering comfort."

Of course. That twat Ryan had been using her as an emotional crutch. But that's not how Shane saw Krista. He wanted her for entirely different things—sexy, naked times, yes—but also for her laughter, her sweet sense of fun and daring. He liked the awe and wonder on her face as she took in a mountaintop view and how she'd catch her breath, still smiling, exhilarated after a steep climb. Always ready for more. Seeing her enjoy herself and knowing he had something to do with it made him feel good. It warmed the cooler areas of his soul, but Shane still struggled with hugs and *there-theres*.

"Comfort feels too much like pity for me," he said, "and I had enough of people's pity last year."

"But offering comfort is what friends do, isn't it? And we're friends, aren't we?"

"Yeah, we're friends." He kissed her neck then. Partly because he couldn't resist it any longer, and partly because he wanted them both to be reminded of what their special brand of friendship involved.

Krista leaned into him, but she didn't turn her head, didn't offer her lips. Instead, she lowered her gaze to the shoreline again. Shane went back to simply holding her.

What was she thinking?

And did those thoughts involve certain kinds of feelings that would make everything extra complicated and messy?

But that couldn't be the case, could it? Not so soon anyway. Only this time yesterday, they'd still been two people who barely knew each other, playing pool at the Moose Head Lodge.

And two days before that, she'd been crying over Ryan and Shane had been hoping to get naked with Zoey, thinking she'd be the woman to end his self-imposed celibacy with, not Krista. So didn't that mean that what his and Krista's *friendship* boiled down to now was what it had boiled down to this morning? Their remaining time together should only involve good times, sexy times, fun and laughter, and pushing the real world aside.

Until Sunday.

Krista must've come to the same conclusion, because still she didn't say anything. And she would've done, wouldn't she? It wasn't like her not to spill the thoughts in her head out into the air.

So, as the sky turned orange in front of them, Shane pulled Krista closer to his body and wrapped his arms around her. When she leaned back into him, he rested his head on hers, sealing the deal on their unspoken agreement to get back on track with being *friends*.

"You wanna hear what else happened on my wedding day?" he said.

"Your sister smashed a cream cake in your would-be mother-in-law's face?"

"We didn't get as far as the cake." Shane chuckled at the image though, and just as he'd hoped, addressing the issue of his awful wedding day straight on eased the tension. "So, Claire was still off on one outside on the street, exchanging insults with Fiona's aunt, who apparently said something about me maybe not being enough for her niece. I don't know. And I don't care, but Claire wouldn't have it. She ended up backing Fiona's aunt against this fountain. . ."

"Oh no."

"Yep, she fell in. And that's when all hell broke loose. Dad told me months later that he'd had to drag Claire away, kicking and screaming like a four-year-old, before anyone else ended up soaked."

Krista giggled. The sound warmed his soul and righted the ground beneath his feet. It was freeing to laugh about a day that he'd once believed had destroyed his whole life.

"I like your sister," she said.

"Claire needs her head examined." But he liked her heaps too, and he couldn't have survived those weeks after without her help—or rather her nagging and hassling to stop drinking, to stop sleeping around, and take control of his life again.

Claire had bridged the gap between the mess he'd been and the worry Mum and Dad had for him. After causing the shitshow with the press, she'd also helped deflect the many comments on his social media. It was only afterwards that he'd found out what social media trolls had written about him—*McDermit, what a loser. . . Take your head out of the water, dude. . . How could you not know your fiancée was getting off with another man? Are you blind or stupid?*

But now, as he held Krista and watched the sun set, all the crap of last year eased from Shane's body. There were no more dark clouds. No more ghosts of girlfriends past between them.

"I'm sorry I upset you," he said. "Can we go back to enjoying ourselves?"

She relaxed into him. "We already have."

THE SUN SLIPPING BEHIND the mountains painted the sky orange and purple. Wisps of deep red swirled amongst pink clouds, reflecting in the lake, and together with Shane's warm arms around her, Krista was reminded to enjoy the moment. In the pool, immersed in warm water and drifting on the surface next to Shane, she'd never felt happier. Why ruin that happiness now by arguing? Or digging over a past that no longer really mattered?

There was also no point overthinking and trying to second-guess how this vacation *thing* they were currently having would all pan out. Discussions about relationships never got her anywhere with Ryan. It was better to live for the moment.

And the evening was too beautiful to be tarnished by what she'd learned about Shane.

So what if he'd once been in love—*for nearly ten years!*—and been about to get married? It was *his* heart that had been broken, not hers. *His* dreams that had been shattered.

What must that feel like?

To not be living the future he'd planned to live this time last year. To have the woman he'd planned it with betray him so terribly.

Krista had had a taste of that kind of betrayal and disappointment when she'd caught Ryan kissing Zoey. But Shane had experienced it all on an entirely different scale.

His life must truly have been knocked sideways. But he'd rebuilt that "excellent" life now. He was proceeding, full speed ahead. Not licking his wounds and feeling sorry for himself.

She understood now why he'd refused her comfort. Okay, he could have done it more subtly, more diplomatically, but he'd apologized, and his arms around her now were making amends for his bluntness.

It was a good thing that they'd had this minor falling out. Those heated words had sparked a new fire between them. One that blazed a little brighter, more intense. She felt closer to him now. He was less of a stranger again.

She knew a little more about his life.

But where and how did Krista—a vacation fling—fit into it all? She didn't know.

And that was okay, wasn't it? Because Shane had made no promises. He hadn't lied to her; he hadn't played any games. He'd given her the choice to walk away. But she'd wanted his body, his pleasure, and she'd given hers just as willingly.

It wasn't his fault that she now wanted the rest of him, too. The whole boyfriend-girlfriend package.

And that's really why she'd gotten upset. Girlfriends comforted boyfriends, and vice versa. But he hadn't seen it like that.

Clearly, the whole Shane McDermit boyfriend package wasn't up for grabs—and even if it was, it would only be for a patchy six months, in between his grueling training schedule and studies, before he returned to Australia.

Was it even possible for any kind of decent relationship to flourish between the gaps and cracks of his busy life?

Night was falling around them now. It was getting late. Shane's hot lips grazed over her neck again, dropping little kisses here and there at the sensitive spots around her ears. Giggling, laughing, wanting more, Krista curled into him, offering her lips and receiving his. As they kissed, his right hand ran across her breasts, her stomach, her hips, and then slid down to massage the sweet, yearning spot between her legs—reminding her of exactly what she'd signed up for.

The fire burned even brighter. Hotter. Crackling and sizzling. Consuming all doubts and *what ifs* and leaving the question of *what will happen Sunday?* simmering beneath the flames.

Chapter 19

THE CORAL PEAK TRAIL, ten miles outside of Jasper, was steep, hard, and rough. It was Saturday morning. The last full day of their holiday. This was their last hike, and Shane could tell Krista was struggling with the climb. Every twenty meters or so, she'd pause and take a few breaths.

"You okay?"

She nodded and carried on. A few minutes later, they were faced with a thirty-meter scramble to the last ridge, where they'd finally get to the *top of the world* views they'd been working towards for the past two hours.

Taking another deep breath, Krista eyed the rocky trail ahead. "Do you think it's safe?"

"A hundred percent," he told her, even though from where they were standing, the trail looked almost vertical. Shane's thighs screamed just looking at it. The loose scree and stones would be fatiguing and uncomfortable on their hands and knees. But apart from a few scuffs and scrapes here and there, they weren't in any immediate danger. He didn't take risks—especially with safety—and there were plenty of trees and roots to rest on and grab, should they need to if they missed their footing.

The trail was also busy, with plenty of other hikers of all ages attempting the same climb.

Still, he didn't want Krista to feel pressured. "We can turn back if you want to."

Her gaze drifted to just below the peak, to where that ridge they were aiming for still looked so far away. She looked tired.

Their hike yesterday hadn't been so steep, but at over thirty K, it had been the longest they'd done. They hadn't been able to resist the meadows, extending their hike more and more to see as much of the peaceful surroundings as possible.

"Krista? Let's turn back."

"No, it's okay." With a deep breath, she pushed on. "We've come this far."

"You sure?"

"I'm sure. Let's do this." She wrapped her hands around the thin trunk of a tree that grew out amongst the rocks. Placing her foot on a well-carved-out foothold, she stepped up and began her scramble.

Shane did the same behind her, following her path up. When she paused, he paused. When she climbed, he climbed, always scouring the route ahead of them, even though Krista seemed to instinctively know where to place her hands and feet. She was a natural-born climber. Fit, strong, determined.

Clutching at rocks and roots sticking half out of the ground, they continued to scramble, keeping their pace and momentum until finally, a few minutes later, they reached the ridge.

"Man, that hurt," Krista gasped, dropping to the stony ground. She blew out a long breath as her trance-like gaze traveled across the jagged line of mountain peaks as far as the eye could see. Her face was red and sweaty, her hair all messed up and flicking in the wind, but she'd never looked prettier. Her delicate features were somehow more pronounced now that he'd just witnessed her strength and grit.

"But it was worth every second," she said, her eyes sparkling with wonder and exhilaration. "This is just beyond awesome!"

Aware that he was staring at her more than at the incredible view, Shane dragged his gaze away from the side of her face. They were eyeline not only with ice-capped peaks but also big, fat clouds rolling by.

"We're on top of the world," he said, and then he felt it again. That swirling, aching feeling in his chest. He hadn't been able to shift it for two days, not since the night they'd argued by the lake. Nerves, excitement, worry, and happiness. The feeling increased every time he looked at Krista and went off the charts when he thought about tomorrow.

After they'd kissed and made up at Medicine Lake, it was like an invisible shield had deflected any mention of their normal world, leaving them cocooned and safe to simply *be* inside their holiday bubble.

But tomorrow. . .

He didn't want to say goodbye to Krista. But what about his new life plan? It had been going so well, and he couldn't risk it all on Krista's pretty face and sexy times—no matter how much he liked her, nor how good she made him feel.

Too risky.

And Shane didn't take risks—not with his safety and certainly not with his heart. He couldn't have that trashed again, not when he'd busted a gut to regain his focus after Fiona.

And in a few months' time, he'd be living 12,500 kilometers away in Sydney. Back to training hard for his last Olympics and working all other hours in between to get his new career off the ground.

There was no time for taking risks, no time to mess about and get distracted from his goals. No time to wonder if he'd be lied to and betrayed again, back to always having one eye on the door, waiting for someone to walk through it and say, "She's not coming."

·♥·♥·♥·♥·♥·

LATER THAT NIGHT, IN the campground that was beginning to feel like home, Shane stared at the darkened forest surrounding him. Stars twinkled in between the treetops, and moonlight tinted the edge of leaves and branches. Everything felt and looked so crisp and clear here, even at night.

He wished he could say the same about his thoughts.

Should he and Krista start dating in Vancouver?

Would she even want to continue seeing him?

It felt like she would. So what did he have to lose? He should ask her, but every time he thought to bring up the subject, his wedding day came crashing back to mind.

What do you mean she's not coming?

She's just messaged me. Jonno, his best man, had stood in the doorway of that little side room in the church. *She said she'd messaged you and to check your phone.*

What groom checks his damn phone on his wedding day? When everyone in his damn life who could possibly want to speak to him was sitting in a church waiting for the damn show to begin?

But confusion was quickly swapped by dread, and the dread by disbelief.

Fiona was crying when he called her. *I can't do this. I'm sorry.*

And then she told him why.

Two fucking years!

He'd had no idea.

But then all the times she'd gone away for a night with work, or a training course, or to see an old friend. . .

I tried to break it off with him, she'd said. *But I love him more. . .*

Fragments of the past echoed in the forest, rebounding off the trees as Shane stared into the night. He'd fallen short of whatever bar Fiona had set. He'd lost the race. He hadn't been able to keep her.

That was certainly one side of his agony. But there were other sides too. The fact that she'd lied to him. And he'd fallen for it. For two years.

There were no prizes for guessing that he was still shell-shocked by what Fiona had revealed that awful day. And how those revelations had blown the foundations of his world apart. How could she have done that to him? He'd been in love with her for so long—he thought he knew her inside out—and believed that she loved him back.

How did he truly know what people felt about him? Would—and could—a good friend like Mikey Adams stab him in the back one day too? Could his own sister turn against him one day and do the same? Shane couldn't believe that would ever be the case, but then, that's what he would have said about Fiona too. Never in a million years would he have imagined her capable of leading a double life like that.

Now, walking through life was like walking through a minefield. Shane couldn't really know what could blow up in his face until it did. So it was best to keep on safer paths, wasn't it? It was best to map out his future, stick to the plan. The explosion-free route.

Krista's light footsteps sounded behind him, quieting the echoes of his past. His whole body went on high alert, and his soul screamed for the comfort he'd refused the other evening.

"What are you looking at out here?" she asked.

"Nothing, really. Just enjoying the night." And it was their last one together, so there was no point in dredging up the past and telling her that what he'd really been looking at was his future.

And whether he was brave enough to carve out a place for her in it.

The swirl in his gut gave him his answer. A simple, *You can't.*

Because not only would they be living on different continents in six months' time, but also, looking out into the night had made Shane remember how fragile the tether of a relationship could be. How it could so easily snap and send him spiraling out of control again.

Behind him, Krista wrapped her arms around his waist and rested her head against his back. Like a warm blanket, the heat from her body seeped into his, soothing and calming.

"Coral Peak was impressive, eh?" she said.

"It was out of this world. My thighs though. . ."

"Want me to see to them again?"

He smiled. "You see to mine, I'll see to yours."

"I like the sound of that," she said, sniggering behind him. "Although it's not just my thighs that are aching. I ache in other places too."

"Is that so?"

"Uh-huh."

Shane turned and put his arms around her, and when he kissed her on the lips, a different vision of his future flashed in his mind.

Would it work?

Could he risk his heart again?

"Krista, do you want to. . ."

See where this thing goes when we're back in Vancouver? Go out for a meal and a movie like a real couple?

The questions were bubbling up inside him, but he bottled them. *Gutless wonder.*

"Do I want to. . . what?" Still in his arms, Krista looked up at him, but the words stuck in his throat.

Training! Studying! New life plan! The minefield! Boom!

"Do you want to. . . grab breakfast at the service station tomorrow? It'll take an hour to charge up the car, but we'll have time before heading back to Banff."

"Oh, right. Yeah, that would be awesome."

He searched her face for signs of disappointment, but her perky smile and the *come to bed* tug of his T-shirt told him all he needed to know.

Krista knew the score.

She understood how holiday flings worked.

So it was about time that he understood it too.

GRAB BREAKFAST?

That's *all* Shane had been thinking about?

Yeah, right.

Krista didn't believe it for one second, but she'd promised herself at the lake the other night to live in the moment, so she wasn't going to pursue Shane's thoughts now. There would be time for talking tomorrow *and* when they got back to Vancouver.

It didn't matter that Shane still hadn't mentioned any plans beyond breakfast. Nor that he hadn't mentioned her flight home. With Ryan. But then, neither had she.

Was he waiting for her to say something?

Was that why he was staring out into the night?

Well, she had news for him. Up on Coral Peak today, she'd come to her own conclusions about what they should do tomorrow morning. She'd made her own plans. Plans that had been simmering ever since Medicine Lake. She'd had enough of *waiting* for a relationship to happen. So, grabbing that bull by the balls, she'd tell Shane exactly what she wanted to happen between them.

But not tonight.

"Come," she said. "Let's go to bed."

Tonight was just about them. To enjoy and absorb and remember. There'd be no talk of the future.

Because really, it could go either way with Shane. He was so hard to read sometimes. So hard to really see into his soul, which he didn't bare very often. And if he ever did give her a glimmer of what he was feeling inside—like the other night at the hot springs—he'd close up and move on too quickly for her to properly figure out what was going on.

Second-guessing how he felt about her was near on impossible. He could say, *Yeah, sure, let's see where this thing goes,* or he could blow her off with a, *Well, you see Krista, I'm kinda busy and this holiday was nice n' all. . . but, no thanks. It's over.*

If that would be his answer, how could she then spend the night with him in this dark camping ground? Or sit in a car for two hours with him as he drove her back to Banff?

After all, Shane was a guy who'd been jilted at the altar. He'd been lied to and betrayed. *Once bitten, twice shy.* She could understand why his shell had hardened.

But was this connection they had—that sparked and sizzled and made *her* feel like she'd known him forever—enough to bring him out of that shell?

Chapter 20

THE NEXT MORNING, AT the service station just off the Icefields Park-way, Krista sipped her coffee, admiring Shane's physique as he walked away to check on the car. Last night, when they'd made love and touched each other in all the right places, in all the right ways, Krista knew today wouldn't be the end of them. She'd never felt so in-sync like this with anyone before, and after their final kiss goodnight, she'd snuggled against his chest and closed her eyes—her decision made.

Today, she wouldn't be getting on her flight home. Instead, she'd set off on the ten-hour drive back to Vancouver with Shane.

Not that he knew it yet.

She wanted to surprise him with this last summer vacation treat by booking them a room somewhere special and romantic. Just the thought of sleeping with him in an actual bed was exciting enough. She didn't have any clients booked in tomorrow, so her manager wouldn't mind if she took another day off. Now, all she had to do was find a hotel somewhere near the halfway mark in Revelstoke. She switched on her phone then gazed out of the window, trying to imagine Shane's reaction when she told him. A smile curled her lips. Would the hotel shower be big enough for the two of them?

Krista's phone beeped in her hand, startling her out of her steamy daydreams and back to what she'd been doing.

Right. Searching for a hotel. She wanted—

Her gaze hit on a text message from Ryan. Then another. And another. She hadn't turned her phone on in days, and now all his messages popped up like one long stream of consciousness.

`I've seen the pictures of you and Shane. Are you seriously a thing now?`

`Where does this leave us?`

`I miss you.`

Eh? Krista couldn't believe what she was reading.

`I want us to be together. Now is the right time for us. I love you.`

Finally. Ryan had said the words she'd once been so desperate to hear.

Krista lowered her phone then caught Shane staring at her.

"What is it?" he asked.

"Ryan messaged me." She read out the texts, so surprised that she started to laugh. "Oh, my god, Shane! Your plan, the bet—those photos of us… It actually worked!" *Was posting a photo on social media all it took to make Ryan see her as more than just a friend? Was he really that shallow?* "He really did get jealous!" she added.

When Shane didn't say anything, Krista looked up. He stared at her a long moment then blinked and smiled.

"I'm very happy for you," he said.

Wha— "You're happy? Because Ryan is in love with me?"

"I always knew my plan would work. You've got what you've always wanted now." Shane tapped the table. "So, you ready to head back to Banff?"

"What? Now?"

"Of course. I've got a long drive ahead, and I'd like to make a start on it sooner rather than later. I'll go and pay for our breakfast and see you back at the car." He strode to the counter, one hand already whipping out his wallet from his back pocket.

Krista gawped after him.

Was he for real?

Her thighs were still aching from the amount of hot, mind-blowing sex they'd had, and he was in a hurry to drive her back to Banff?

Grabbing her phone off the table, she stomped after him. Shane was already on the forecourt, heading toward his car without even looking behind him to see where she was.

"Shane!" she called out. "What the—"

"Kris! Krista!"

Krista whirled round. A car full of people shouting out her name was pulling up alongside the diner.

"We found you!"

Oh, my god! It was Ryan and a bunch of others from work, all hanging out of the car's windows, waving and cheering and turning every damn head toward her. Ryan burst out and threw his arms around her, lifting her off her feet.

"Did you get my messages?" he said, swinging her around and around. Her head spun, she lost her bearings. "I've missed you."

"Ryan, what—"

Before she could turn away, he smacked a kiss on her lips then pulled her into a tight hug. Krista's head spun further.

Everyone refueling or charging their vehicles was staring at her—so too were the dozens and dozens of people sitting outside by the diner, sipping coffees and eating waffles as they took in the show.

"I'm—"

"I've been an idiot, Kris. I've missed you so much." Then his wet lips smacked against hers again.

She jerked her head away. "No, Ryan. . ."

But all their co-workers were whooping and clapping, like at the ending of one of those sweet and fluffy rom-coms she always enjoyed. Except there was nothing sweet and fluffy and enjoyable about Ryan's arms around her and everyone watching. It was awkward and embarrassing and so not what she wanted.

"Ryan," she said again and started to ease herself out of his arms, but was struck by the joy and happiness on his face.

"I love you, Krista," he said, his eyes were almost heart-shaped. "We've spent days looking for you, and then we figured we'd find you here if McDermit had to charge up his car before driving back."

"But Ryan," she whispered, "listen, I. . . The thing is, I'm—"

"Hey, lovers!" Darren called out.

"We've gotta hit the road, kids," someone else shouted. "We've got a plane to catch."

The group approached. Krista smiled at everyone then asked how they were. What else could she do? They all seemed so excited to see her, and whatever adventure they'd been on to find her was making them all laugh and whoop.

"I can't believe our detective work actually paid off," Darren said, throwing his arm around her too. Engulfed in this group of people she had to see every day at work, Krista plastered a smile on her face. "Ryan's been calling the shots, haven't you, Ry? He wouldn't let us rest until he found you."

But if they'd put so much effort into finding her, they must've missed out on so much of their vacation!

"Really, guys, you shouldn't have. . ." *But where was Zoey?* "Where's everyone else?" she asked.

"In Banff."

"Sergeant Ryan wanted us to form a splinter group. . ."

"He's been on a mission."

"It's been a quest, for sure!"

They were all speaking at once now, all laughing, bantering and congratulating each other. Krista laughed along with them too. She was so steamrolled and bamboozled and embarrassed, she didn't know what else to do.

Ryan put his arm around her again, but just like his kiss a few seconds go, it felt so wrong. So unnatural. All she wanted to do was get to Shane and figure out why he was leaving in such a hurry.

Easing Ryan's arm away from her shoulders, she scanned the service station for Shane.

Then, as if Ryan had read her mind, he asked, "Where's McDermit?"

"I'm here."

Krista's heart jumped. Shane was standing behind her, holding her bags.

He placed them at her feet. A statement that said loud and clear—in front of *every*one—that he didn't want her with him.

"Thanks for the good time, Krista," he said, all chirpy and jolly and not the least bit bothered by this outrageous surprise out of the blue that was making her heart beat so fast she felt like passing out.

"Shane—"

"See you around." Then with a quick nod to the others, he strode to his car, slid in behind the wheel, and drove away.

IT TOOK ALL OF Shane's strength not to shoot down the Icefields Parkway, honking at anyone who'd get in his way.

He should've known that the minute bloody Ryan showed up, Krista would be back at his feet. As she'd stared at her phone, he'd seen how her face had lit up. Her smile was dazzling, her eyes sparkly, and he knew—*just fucking knew*—that she was reading messages from Ryan.

So that dweeb finally had the spine to fess up and tell her he loved her?

And not only that—just as Shane had predicted—he'd also literally swept her off her feet. Shane could've lived without seeing Krista being kissed by another man—a man she'd always wanted—and from the looks of how they were kissing on the forecourt, they belonged together. Surrounded by their cheering friends. *And they lived happily ever after. . .*

Well, it's what Krista had wanted all along, wasn't it? Ryan confessing his undying love for her. So, who was Shane to get in the way of that? She'd planned this whole trip to the Rockies so she could be with that pretty boy.

Strewth almighty.

Did Krista really think someone like Ryan would make her happy?

Shane wasn't going to hang around to find out because—*Boom!*—another minefield had just blown up in his face.

Poor Shane, missing out...

He'd fallen short again.

The Nearly Man.

But no way was he hanging around for anyone to say that to him now.

Instead, he'd hauled his poker face on and got the hell away. What else could he do? Watch the Cute Couple Show, like everyone else at that damn service station, clap and whoop? No thanks.

Tearing down the highway, mountains blurring past, he turned his music up full blast, just like he did before a race when he needed to focus, and zoned out everything except the road ahead.

In twelve hours, he'd be back in Vancouver. He had training. He had studying to do.

He had his new life plan.

Which didn't include Krista in it.

Chapter 21

Throughout the whole flight back to Vancouver, Ryan had been so attentive. He'd barely glanced at Zoey, who'd sat at the front of the airplane with the half of the group who didn't go on Sergeant Ryan's mission to track Krista down.

At the back, Krista could hear Zoey laughing, catching glimpses of her shiny raven hair flicking this way and that as she talked. Ryan still hadn't said anything about making out with her in the hotel gardens, and Krista hadn't asked. She was still in shock.

How could Shane have left her like that?

She wanted to call him. But despite knowing his sexual preferences, she didn't know his number.

How very Lisa of her.

But out in the Rockies, Shane had been by her side 24/7. There'd been no need to swap numbers. Adding Shane to her contacts list was yet another real-world thing that Krista had planned to do this morning—like the hotel room reservation in Revelstoke.

Like telling Shane they should carry on seeing each other.

This reverse order of things—of sex before dating—had thrown her. She'd never been the *jump into bed* kind of woman. She'd always gotten to know her bed partner well before they'd ever hit the sheets. But wasn't that just the thing? Krista had *felt* like she knew Shane. After the ice had broken between them at Lake Louise—after he'd seen her at her worst—she'd felt so comfortable with him, like she'd known him forever.

So what did that say about trusting her feelings?

The argument by the lake had been a warning, but she'd been too swept up with the whole *live for the moment* vacation romance thing to take notice.

A bag of cookies appeared under her nose. Darren was passing them around. Even though her stomach was inside out, Krista managed to eat one. And she managed to laugh and banter with her friends. No one had asked what she'd gotten up to with Shane. Maybe because she'd already nipped any gossip in the bud by droning on about switchbacks, and meltwater streams, glaciers, and scrambling up steep mountain slopes.

Or maybe they didn't ask because Ryan was sitting next to her and everyone now thought they were a happy couple.

God, what a mess!

How would she tell Ryan she no longer wanted to date him? It wasn't in her to be blunt. It wasn't in her to hurt his feelings, and she didn't want their workplace environment to become awkward.

And what about Shane's social media? Had he taken down the photos of them together?

She should take a look as soon as she was able to, but really, she didn't have the strength right now to deal with the crap people posted online.

Truth was, no one but her and Shane would ever know how they'd explored every naked inch of each other's bodies. No one would ever know they'd made love in the wilderness, amongst the trees and under the stars. All that passion, dissipated into the wild, gone forever. So much for everlasting love. So much for romance. It was just sex. Casual, *doesn't mean a thing* sex.

And now what?

As the plane landed at YVR, Krista unclipped her belt, retrieved her bags, and drifted with the hordes out of the airport, chewing over that same question. *Now what?*

What was next for Krista Gervais?

Of course, she'd run into Shane at the center. He'd catch her using the men's washrooms again, or spilling gel on the floor, or shouting at one of Lisa's ex-hook ups across the parking lot. And there'd be no trace of that Rocky Mountain heat that had once glowed between them.

He'd put that fire out when he'd dumped her bags at her feet.

". . . then Mom told me she missed her therapy session," Ryan said beside her. They were on the Skytrain now, alone. They'd said goodbye to the rest of their group at the airport and had started the last part of their exceedingly long journey home. Ryan would get off at Olympic Village, and Krista would carry on to Yaletown. The minutes ticked by. "Tomorrow, I'm going with her to make sure she attends."

Krista went back to staring out of the window.

"Krista?"

"Hmm?"

"Are you okay? You don't seem yourself."

Because she wasn't hanging on his every word and offering endless advice and support over the latest drama with his mother?

Irritation spiked. "What did Zoey have to say about your mom?" She speared him with a knowing look.

Ryan's face fell—not in a guilty, *I've been busted* way, but more a, *Shit, I really screwed up* kinda way. "Kris, I—"

"I saw you kissing in the hotel gardens."

"I'm sorry." As he dragged his fingers into the thick waves of his hair, his perfectly manicured eyebrows knitted together. "I was going to tell you. I just didn't know how."

She snorted and went back to looking out of the window.

"I figured that's why you went with Shane, but you didn't say anything, so I—"

"Forget it."

"She doesn't mean anything to me."

"It's fine," she snapped in a way that said it wasn't fine at all.

But Krista didn't want to have this conversation now. She was too tired, too angry. And too frickin' confused by how little she cared about Ryan and Zoey. Such a change of heart shocked her. How could her feelings for Ryan fade so quickly? If she blew hot, cold, and indifferent like this, how could she ever trust her feelings for a man ever again?

But right now, she was too raw from Shane telling her to hit the road to care about anything. With a heavy sigh, she leaned her head back and hoped Ryan would get the message that she didn't want to talk.

No such luck.

"You're upset with me," he said.

"No, I'm not." *I'm upset with Shane.*

"I'm not sure how to explain what happened with Zoey," Ryan continued. "I guess I got carried away in the moment. The night before, after you went to your room, she'd been all over me, and yeah, it was fun. She texted me the next morning, asking to meet alone in the gardens before breakfast, so I—"

"The next morning? You didn't sleep with her?"

"No," Ryan choked. "You know I wouldn't do that."

Krista sank into her seat. A sexy vacation fling definitely wasn't in Ryan's DNA, but neither had it been in hers—until one damn, annoying Australian out in the wilderness had roused her innermost desires.

The train slowed mercifully into the next station.

"This is your stop, Ryan." She turned to the window. "See you at work."

·♥·♥·♥·♥·♥·

THIRTY MINUTES LATER, KRISTA pressed her ear to the door of her apartment, listening for signs of Lisa with a man. Too many times she'd walked in on half-dressed men or tripped over shoes and discarded clothes in the hall. But tonight of all nights, Krista needed her apartment quiet, and if that meant kicking a naked guy out of Lisa's bed, she'd damn well do it. She knocked loudly and turned her key.

"Lisa! I'm coming in, so get dressed and tell whoever you've got in there to pull his pants back on and ship the hell out."

She dumped her bags in the lounge then stopped dead when she saw Lisa sitting up straight on the sofa, dressed in a pink robe and a face pack. *Sunday night.* Of course. Lisa's pampering night. Krista had lost track of days.

"What the hell's gotten into you?" Lisa asked, the clay or mud, whatever the hell that was on her face, crinkled at the corners. "It's good to see you so well rested and relaxed after your vacation."

"Huh." Krista dropped her keys and phone on the coffee table then slumped on the sofa next to her sister. She grabbed the remote and stabbed it toward the TV, flicking through channels full of crap until she could no longer ignore Lisa's eyes boring into the side of her head. "What?"

Lisa's eyebrows shot up, cracking the mask over her forehead. "Still no sex, eh?"

"Oh, please. Is that all you think about? Sex is so overrated. And men? Jesus Murphy, Lisa. Why do you go to such efforts for them?" Krista waved her hands over Lisa's pampering kit—nail varnish and moisturizing bars for this and that, all laid out neatly on a tray. "Men aren't worth it."

"Firstly, I do this"—Lisa waved her arms over all the beauty paraphernalia—"for myself. I like it. I enjoy it. And secondly, do you want to tell me what, or who, has crawled up your ass?"

Krista switched off the TV and slung the remote so hard it bounced off the sofa and onto the floor. Trying to contain the explosion inside her, she folded her arms tightly across her chest. How could she even begin to assess the feelings and emotions racing through her? They were all jangled up and mis-wired, short circuiting so bad that she was blowing fuse after fuse after fuse. Her whole body crackled and hissed with anger and resentment and betrayal and...sadness.

A tear rolled down her cheek.

"Oh, Kris. What did he do to you?" Lisa squeaked and grabbed her hand, her eyes wide and fearful through the holes in her mask. "Did that Shane McDermit force—?"

"What? No!" Krista blinked away her tears. "No! Of course not. Shane wouldn't. . . No, he'd never do anything like that." *He gave me choices and options and the best vacation—and orgasms—ever.*

The memory of Shane's gentle, sensual ways made the tears come back. He'd been so nice and caring, so hot and sexy, so. . . damn perfect. And they'd gotten on well as friends too, hadn't they? So, why the rush to get rid of her?

She sniffed back another bout of tears. "Shane is a loser."

"Aw, c'mon Kris. Dating losers is *my* job, not yours." Lisa nudged her knee, but the humor in her voice didn't work. Another tear rolled down Krista's cheek. "Please tell me what happened?"

"Everything and nothing." The dam broke. Krista sobbed, and the next thing she knew, Lisa's arm was around her, pulling her in for a hug. The contact made her cry even more. Throughout their lives, it had always been Krista hugging Lisa—during bad teenage breakups, missed grades, friendship struggles, and grief for Grandma—but not once had it ever been this way around.

The world had tipped upside down, and Krista hated the mess she'd become as much as she loved the comfort her sister was offering.

"So, I'm guessing something did happen between you and Shane, eh?"

Krista swallowed back her tears and nodded, and then her phone buzzed into life on the coffee table in front of them. Ryan's name flashed up on the screen.

"Aren't you gonna answer?" Lisa asked. The many times Krista's heart had sung whenever he called flooded her already confused mind. This time last week, she'd've raced to answer his call, but now. . .

Her phone buzzed and buzzed then stopped.

The room fell so silent that Krista could hear Lisa breathing. Soft little gasps of air catching in her throat, as if she was trying to choose the right words.

In the end, Lisa said, "Do you wanna talk about it?"

Krista shook her head. Talking to Lisa about men would be like talking to Shane about love. One woman—or man—was much like any other, right? That's what they believed.

Krista's heart sank further.

Because maybe one day, she'd end up believing it too.

Chapter 22

WATER SLUICED OFF SHANE'S body, and his heart beat out of his chest. He reached the side wall and, sucking air back into his burning lungs, turned to Mikey in the next lane. "Let's go again."

"Wha—"

"Again." Shane pushed off the side of the pool and cleared the first ten meters under water. His five-month-long training program—in preparation for the Pan Pacifics in December—didn't start until tomorrow. But, god, he'd needed to swim this morning! And he'd known he'd find Mikey here dead-on six a.m. too.

Surfacing, Shane's arms sliced through the water, his feet kicking. Mechanical movements as natural to him as breathing and walking. He reached the other side—and Mikey was already there. Fuck. The guy was fast. A freaking machine. Shane pushed back under the water, swimming harder, faster, until his fingers struck the opposing wall again. Mid-turn, ready for another length, something underwater pushed into his leg.

It was Mikey's foot.

"What's gotten into you?" he said. Water sprayed from Mikey's mouth, his breathing hard and ragged like Shane's. "You've been in a shitty mood all morning."

Damn right he had. After getting the hell out of the Rockies, he'd driven solidly for six hours, stopped at a service station to charge up his car and tank himself up with coffee, and then driven six hours more. And the patchy few hours of sleep he'd grabbed when he'd arrived back at his apartment wasn't the only thing scratching at his nerves.

Shane sank to the bottom of the pool, but not even the underwater quiet gave him any respite from his raging thoughts.

Krista and Ryan.

Kissing.

Everyone cheering.

Whoop-de-fucking-do.

Okay. So, back on that service station forecourt, it had been Ryan who'd made the first move, but the fact that Krista hadn't exactly pushed him away had been chewing Shane up inside something chronic. What had been going through her mind when that pretty boy swung her off her feet? Had she been weighing up her options—trying to choose who she wanted?

Like Fiona had done for two years.

With his head about to explode, Shane came up for air.

"You wanna go again?" Mikey asked. He'd pulled off his goggles and was watching him with steady, challenging eyes. "Because if it'll help you shift whatever's gotten you so riled, I'm good for another race."

No shit. Of course Mikey would be good for another race. He was young and had superhuman powers in the pool. Shane pulled off his own goggles and wiped his eyes. He'd never been jealous of Mikey. *Never!* But today, he felt like punching his friend in the jaw just because. . . because. . . fuck it. Just because he was the only guy around to punch.

"Let's hit the weights." Shane sprang out of the pool and grabbed his towel off the bench.

"So I see that a week hiking in our great outdoors did you a world of good," Mikey said, as he followed him out of the pool. "And you say you didn't end up asking Zoey to join you?"

"Nope."

"So who did you ask?"

"No one." Shane pushed through the door of the changing room. If Mikey couldn't be bothered to look on his social media more than once in a blue moon, it wasn't Shane's job to fill him in. "So you sorted out that sponsorship deal with your dad?"

"Yeah, Dad arranged it. Howie, my agent, finalized the contract." Mikey reached for a fresh towel off a hook on the side. "So, whoever you took hiking was a headache, right?"

Damn, the change of subject didn't work. "How do you know I didn't go alone?"

"Because I figured you would've said."

"Well, I don't want to talk about it."

"Yeah, I figured that much already too, buddy," Mikey said, pulling on a T-shirt. "It's a beautiful morning. Instead of weights, let's run around Stanley Park."

"Great idea." Shane snatched up his shorts and running shoes, and to his relief, Mikey didn't mention the Rockies again. They finished dressing in silence then headed outside and up along Beach Avenue.

Monday morning commuters were busily walking and cycling to their offices. Traffic beeped and rolled by. Sunshine sparkled on the water of English Bay, bringing to mind the lakes of the Rockies he and Krista had hiked last week.

He still couldn't quite believe what had happened yesterday morning at that service station. Still couldn't believe that Krista would forget all about what they'd shared together and leap into Ryan's arms without a second thought.

But then, Shane hadn't believed Fiona could cheat on him for two bloody years either. That day at the church, he hadn't believed that she'd meant any of the words he was hearing.

I'm sorry, Shane. I love him more.

Shane picked up his pace. Beside him, Mikey did the same. They turned right down Chilco Street, heading toward Coal Harbour. When they got to the 0km marker of the Stanley Park Seawall path, Shane cast a sideways glance at Mikey. Mikey side-eyed him back, and soon they were locked in an unspoken race, overtaking walkers and joggers, dodging roller-skaters and anyone else who got in their way.

The nine km path ran along the water's edge. After his drills in the pool, Shane would often run it as a post-training workout. The scenery was magnificent. But today, Krista's face lighting up with delight as she read Ryan's love texts was all he could see.

And all he could feel was a constant gnawing in his core. Although another man's mouth on Krista's was definitely chewing Shane up inside, what chewed him more was what a gutless, chicken-shitty coward he'd been. Why hadn't he been brave enough to tell Krista he wanted to continue seeing her? Why hadn't he told her how he'd felt that last night in the Rockies, when he'd been gazing out into the night, lonely and scared of getting hurt again?

But wouldn't Krista still have chosen Ryan anyway?

And shouldn't Shane be happy that she had? After all, his new life plan didn't include women. He was the one who'd said, *No thinking*, and wouldn't even entertain the thought of starting something more with her.

Dammit, he was so confused! His confusion had made him act like such a shithead at the service station too, giving Krista her bags back like she'd meant nothing to him. He'd been too pissed off and afraid at the time to stick around. Too worn out with his hang-ups from the past to put up a fight for her.

Propelled by misery and anger, Shane pumped his arms and legs harder. Mikey was right next to him, but by the 8km mark, Shane dug deeper. He found that pot of energy that made him one of Australia's top athletes and got to the last marker three strides ahead of his friend. He'd won the stupid race, but what a joyless, pointless victory it was.

Pain shot through his legs and his chest, and both he and Mikey were panting and coughing like sick dogs.

You should've told her how you feel.

And now it's too late.

"Man"—Mikey wheezed, his head hanging between his knees—"do I happen to know this person who's gotten you so pissed?"

"Yeah." Shane swallowed past the burn in his throat. "You're looking straight at him."

By lunchtime, Shane's crappy mood had lifted a little, but his chest still felt like it was going through a shredder. He and Mikey had jog-walked back to the aquatics center, and although they didn't talk about anything in particular apart from training, the slice of normal was comforting.

As he let himself into his apartment, his stomach growling for food, his phone rang in his back pocket. It was Claire.

"Worm! How's it going?"

"Good. Just back from training, and I'm so hungry right now, I might eat this phone." He pushed his front door shut with his foot, dropped his keys on the counter and his gym bag on the floor, then checked the time on the clock on the wall. It was six a.m. in Sydney. "You had a lie-in today?"

"Ha, so funny. Kiri woke me up an hour ago. He's teething. Then Tyler and Sully woke up too. Mark's on early shift, and I'm home alone with only one spoonful of coffee left in the jar."

"Happy days."

Claire yawned. "So how were the Rocky Mountains?"

"Amazing." *But somewhat overshadowed now by messy feelings and past pain. . .* Shane searched his freezer for the lasagna he'd batch-cooked the other week. "Apart from not letting you sleep, how're those brats of yours?"

"We can hear you, Uncle Shane!"

Shane rolled his eyes at the high-pitched squeaking in the background. "It serves you right for eavesdropping." But despite his low mood, his nieces' giggling tugged a smile on his lips. "Has that mother of yours got me on speaker?"

"Yeah," Claire said. "Got you on hands free while I make breakfast, so no effs and jeffs, okay?"

"As if I would." But as he placed his lasagna in the microwave, he made a mental note to watch his language anyway.

"The kids can't wait to see you at Christmas. You are still coming home then, aren't you?"

"Of course I am." He walked to the living room window, his gaze drifting to the mountains across English Bay that he could just about see peeping over the apartment building next to his. Vancouver was a great city to live in—and he loved the landscape here—but Australia would always be his home.

Which was another reason why his feelings for Krista had unsettled him so much. *Canada was her home.*

"So, you had a good holiday."

"Yep."

"And?"

"And what?"

"That bet you had with your *friend*. . ." Claire accentuated the word. "Who won?"

Agh. The bet. Shane had forgotten he'd told her about it the last time he'd messaged that morning at Lake Louise campground. Krista's cute, fluffy cat pajamas sprang to mind, a sore reminder of how easy and comfortable their new friendship had been last week, just before it had exploded into that hot-as-hell fireball he hadn't known what to do with.

"Me," he said. "I won the bet."

Another joyless, pointless victory.

"You made the other guy jealous? Go you, Mr. Cupid. So they're together now?"

"Yeah," he sighed. Claire went quiet for a few seconds, but when she drew breath to speak again, Shane asked, "How're Mum and Dad?"

"They're okay. So, this—"

"I'll call them later. And Mark's work is going okay?"

"Yeah, yeah, he's good. So, this Krista you hiked with. . . and this guy you helped her get. . ."

Ah, Christ, he should've known Claire wouldn't let it drop.

"It was an idea straight out of a high school rom-com," he said. "A load of nonsense. I've deleted those posts now, so forget it."

"But it worked?"

Shane gritted his teeth. *Ryan swept her off her feet just like Shane said he would.*

"You like her, don't you?"

Choking out a laugh, Shane shrugged, even though Claire wouldn't be able to see him. "She's okay."

"No, I mean, you *like* her. If you didn't, you'd be telling me more details about your little high school game. You love a good prank, especially when it works. Instead, you sound all cagey and. . . *peeved*."

"Peeved?" Shane attempted to laugh again. "Really, Claire, you need to get out more."

"Pot calling the kettle black, Worm." The background clatter in Claire's kitchen faded. "Right, you're off speaker now. So, what happened?"

Knowing he was toast, Shane blew out a long, weary breath.

"The high school rom-com happened," he said, then flopped onto his sofa and told Claire all about Krista. From finding her in the bushes to dumping her bags at her feet.

"Way to go," Claire said. "That must've have made her feel really special."

"But she'd made her choice by then."

"How do you know for sure?"

"Because. . ." Uncertainty clawed at him for a moment then died, killed by the image of a bridegroom left standing at the altar without a bride. "Because I've learned a few things this past year."

"I knew that witch would have something to do with this."

Holding the phone away from his ear, Shane let Claire rip. Ranting about Fiona was one of his sister's favorite steam-busting past times—especially after a night of no sleep.

"And I hope she chokes on that stupid little rat-dog of hers."

"You're starting on Pookie now?" Shane said. "Wow, last night must've been really rough with the kids."

"You hated that yappy creature as much as I did."

But Fiona had loved her brainless Cavapoo. It had been a standing joke between them—one of many. Like the fancy parties she'd dragged him to for her work. As an events' organizer, Fiona used to say she loved showing him off in a tux to her clients, that he looked like James Bond on steroids and was good for business. Her work was one of the reasons they'd bought and moved into the apartment in the Central Business District, overlooking the Opera House and Sydney Harbour, instead of the large house in the suburbs that he'd wanted. A large house built with children in mind.

"It's time to get over Fiona," Shane told his sister now. "You're more hung up on her and what she did than I am."

"That's not true."

"No, you're right. It isn't." Shane couldn't deny it anymore. He'd let Krista go because he was afraid of getting hurt again. *Once bitten, twice shy.* She'd said it herself by Medicine Lake. Would she therefore understand why he'd fled at the service station?

Would she hear him out and let him explain?

But now that she had Ryan, would whatever Shane had to say really matter anymore?

Chapter 23

On Mondays, Krista's shift at the aquatics center started at twelve p.m., but she called her manager to request a personal day, too fatigued to risk running into Shane. Ryan had texted her, asking if she wanted to meet for coffee before their shift, but she'd messaged him back, telling him she was going to spend the day at home.

`Are you skipping work because of what I did with Zoey? Are you OK? I feel terrible enough as it is.`

She told him her personal day had nothing to do with him, but she didn't have the energy to write any comforting words to make him feel any less *terrible*. Truth was, she wanted to be left alone to sort out the tangle in her mind, and she couldn't do that at work. Not when all her co-workers now thought she was dating Ryan. And definitely not when she'd spend the whole time looking over her shoulder for Shane.

`How about dinner Friday night? Or bowling?`

Krista sighed at Ryan's latest message. God, she wished he'd go away.

And that made her feel awful.

Ryan was sweet and kind and gentle. . . but his attention now grated on her nerves.

Too much, too late.

Now, that conviction she'd once had that she and Ryan should be together seemed like it had come from a different person entirely. How could she change her mind so rapidly?

And it wasn't just her mind either. The change of heart, of mind, ran through every cell of her body. It cast a different light on every memory, desire, and daydream she'd ever had about every man she'd ever met and was ever likely to meet—not just Ryan.

Bottom line—Shane, *the jerk*, had ruined every relationship she was ever going to have. Because how could any man compete against him and that Rocky Mountain heat they'd generated?

And that, Kool Krista, is why you should never act on your feelings ever again. Just hard facts and cold truths from now on.

Like bags dumped on a service station forecourt.

Didn't that tell her plain and clear that Shane wasn't interested.

Grabbing her travel bags off her bedroom floor, she sorted out her laundry and stuffed her shoes into her wardrobe. Then she set about tidying her room—and the rest of the apartment. Anything to keep from thinking. But by early afternoon, she'd grown bored of her own miserable company and texted her mom to say she'd go visit her at the coffee shop.

When Krista arrived half an hour later, the lunchtime rush had died down and there was only one person sitting at the corner table, reading a car magazine. *Jonas*. Mom's latest boyfriend. The guy had become a part of the furniture. Didn't he have a life of his own?

"Hey," she said.

"Hey, Krista." Jonas's smile was wide and warm. Crow's feet crinkled the corners of his eyes, and the sunlight streaming through the window caught on the shaggy silver hair around his temples. "How were the Rockies?"

"Good. Thanks. Is Mom around?"

"Hi, sweetie!" Mom walked through from the kitchen at that same moment. "I was looking for more cake boxes out back, but looks like we're out. Jonas, would you mind walking up to Patricia's to get me a few?"

"Sure thing."

"I'll message her to tell her you're on your way."

Jonas got up and walked straight out.

Krista lifted one eyebrow. "What? Is he working for you now?"

"No, he just helps out, makes him feel useful while he waits for a new job."

"Is he actually looking? Or waiting for it to fall from the sky on to his lap?"

"Don't be like that, honey. Jonas is a sweet man. I like him."

Yeah, Mom liked a lot of men.

How did she do that? Shift from one to another without getting attached or hurt or even a little upset? She even remained friends with most of them afterwards, too. Like she had with Dad. Though Krista could barely remember her parents together, they were always amicable and polite to each other.

Krista couldn't imagine being so friendly and relaxed toward Shane. . . or Ryan. Both were irritating the hell out of her right now—Ryan for his over attentiveness, and Shane for his being. . . such a dick.

And both had challenged her long-held beliefs about solid, steady relationships. They shook the earth beneath her feet. Solidness and steadiness didn't sound very passionate. But where was the fun in passion if it wasn't founded on the solid and steady ground she'd always had mapped out for herself? So far, passion alone sucked—or rather, the aftereffects did. That blast of heat and want and need was great while it lasted, but it now left her feeling empty, mixed up, and hurt. Like she'd been used and discarded.

"Oh, sweetie, are you okay?"

Krista looked up and blinked. "Sure, I'm okay."

But Mom's look said she knew differently. "Tell me about your vacation. The other day, Lisa showed me photos on the internet of that hunk you took off hiking with." Mom nudged her elbow and flashed her a saucy smile. "I bet you had a lot of fun with him."

"Ew, Mom, seriously? He's just one of the athletes I work with."

"Whatever you say, sweetie." But when Mom put her arms around her and made her feel five years old again, Krista suspected Lisa had already told her she'd been crying over that particular athlete last night. "Why don't you and Lisa come over for dinner tonight? I'll throw some pizzas in the oven, and we can watch a movie. We'll have a girls' night."

"What about Jonas?"

"I'll get rid of him. He can go stay with his brother."

Mom arranging family time? Wow, I must look really miserable. But Krista snuggled farther into her mother's arms. "Thanks, Mom, that sounds great. I'll text Lisa now to tell her."

She pulled out her phone and saw another message from Ryan.

`I've made reservations at Ciro's for to-`
`morrow night after work. Please Krista, we`
`really need to talk.`

Ryan was right. They did need to talk. Well, not talk exactly, because that suggested yet another discussion.

And what Krista had to tell him wasn't up for debate.

"So, you made this hundred-dollar bet to make Ryan jealous," Mom said, helping herself to another slice of pizza. "But you ended up sleeping with Shane."

"And the sex was just for fun, huh?" Lisa chimed in. She picked a piece of mushroom off her slice and popped it into her mouth with a saucy wink. "About time, sis."

Krista rolled her eyes. She wasn't in the habit of talking about her sex life with Mom and Lisa—probably because she'd never had much of one to talk about—but she'd been so miserable today that she hadn't been able to stop the words from coming. She told them everything that had happened with Shane. Did they understand how she was feeling? Krista wasn't sure, but it was good to get the thoughts and memories out of her head so she could make sense of them.

"Being with Shane *was* fun," she said. "And I know he's been hurt in the past, but I never thought he'd run out on me the way he did when Ryan turned up."

"Whoa, Ryan turned up?"

Krista squeezed her eyes shut, reliving that awful moment. "Ryan turned up with some of the gang, literally swept me off my feet, and kissed me."

"Did Shane see that?" Mom asked.

Krista's eyes flew open. "No. I don't know. Maybe."

But Shane had been at his car, and wouldn't he have said something if he had seen? Something sarcastic or angry or jealous...anything to show that he hadn't liked another man kissing her?

Instead, he'd looked. . . well, calm and composed. And detached.

"If he saw you kissing Ryan, that might explain why he hightailed it out of there."

"But *I* wasn't kissing *him*. *He* was kissing *me*!" Could that really be why Shane had taken off? But surely, if he had seen, he would've known that—after everything they'd done together last week—she didn't want Ryan! And she'd never kiss another man in front of him like that anyway. Who did Shane think she was? Krista shook her head. "Maybe he was just using Ryan as an excuse to end it with me?"

"Maybe," Lisa said. "Maybe not."

"Sounds to me like the first thing you need to do is tell Ryan you no longer want him," Mom said, surprisingly helpful. "Unless of course you want to use him to make Shane jealous."

Okay, perhaps not that helpful.

"Or," Lisa said, "you could hunt Shane down and jump his bones. If he refuses, then at least you'll know how he feels."

Krista balled her napkin and chucked it at her. "Still with the grabbing the bull by the balls, eh?"

"Either that, or you forget all about him." Lisa took a large bite of pizza. "The choice is yours, Kris."

· ❤ · ❤ · ❤ · ❤ · ❤ ·

WHAT A CHOICE!

The next day, although Krista was feeling fortified by her impromptu girls' night, she still didn't think she could jump Shane's bones, not when he'd chucked her bags out of his car, but nor could she forget all about him. Not when her heart and soul were still aching for his touch.

The choice is yours...

She'd spent the whole day at work looking furtively around herself in case she ran into Shane. What would she say to him?

And more importantly, what would *he* say?

Her stomach was in knots, a churning mixture of hurt and anger, longing and desire. So, all day she'd stayed clear of the pool areas and changing rooms, which was why she was currently changing for this dinner date with Ryan in the washrooms behind the main reception area.

Tucked away, she took off her sports gear and pulled on jeans and a simple black top. She didn't want to give Ryan the impression that she'd dressed up—not that he'd noticed much in Banff, the last time she'd dressed up for him—but still, she took the time to do her makeup nicely. The dark circles around her eyes were crying out to be covered up, and a swipe or two of mascara and lip gloss would help lift her spirits.

When she was done, she flicked the comb through her hair then stepped out into the lobby.

And came face-to-face with the man who'd turned her life upside down.

Chapter 24

Her sweet, kissable lips were glossy. Her cheeks flushed, like they'd been after every time they'd made love. And although he'd been itching to bump into her all day, Shane still hadn't been prepared for the slam in his chest when he saw her again.

"Krista." He swallowed hard and gawped like the idiot he was. "Um. . . how's it going?"

"Good. You?"

"Yeah, good." His pulse was racing, lifting his heavy heart. Krista had consumed his thoughts. Not for one waking second had he stopped thinking about her. She'd even run through his dreams at night. This morning, he'd again woken restless and yearning, as if something big was missing from deep inside. But with so many words and emotions and urges bubbling through him, how could he even begin to tell her that he missed her, that he wanted her? And that he was too afraid to admit any of it. "So. . . um. . ."

"So. . . ?" She tilted her chin toward him, but her eyes didn't meet his.

Beside him, Mikey coughed.

Shane blinked, reminded that he wasn't alone. "So, um, yeah. We're finishing our first training session with a run along the Seawall Path to Stanley Park, and..."

A tall, wiry guy with dark, wavy hair came to stand very close to Krista.

Ryan.

The pretty boy was looking straight at him with Keep Off signs in his eyes.

Right. Of course. That's why Krista was all made up after work. *Date night.*

Shane stepped back. "Have a good evening, kids."

Then he marched past the reception desk and ran out into the fresh, evening air.

"Well, at least now I know who you took hiking," Mikey said, keeping a brisk pace behind him.

"Huh," Shane huffed and concentrated on his stride.

They crossed the street to the coastal path along the sandy beaches of English Bay. It was a dull, overcast day, but still the beach was busy. Friends chatting as they sat on the logs, a woman reading a magazine, young families playing in the sand.

"When she's not scowling, Krista's kinda cute," Mikey said.

"She's taken is what she is. She's got the man she wants."

"She didn't look too happy about it. What happened between you out in the Rockies, bud?"

"We hooked up. No big deal."

"Did you have fun?"

"Yeah. A lot of fun."

"Then why does she still look like she hates you?"

Because I practically ran away from her at the service station. . .

Shane stopped running.

"You okay?" Mikey jogged on the spot.

"You're right. She did look at me like she hated me. And why would she do that if she's got Ryan?"

"Um. . ."

"And so why the hell should it matter if I did leave her at the service station?"

"Dude, you're not making much sense."

No, he wasn't. Nothing made sense anymore.

And it was time to do something about it.

·♥·♥·♥·♥·♥·

AFTER WATCHING SHANE LITERALLY run away from her—*again*—Krista barged through the main doors and out onto the street, needing some serious big air to steady her nerves.

Ryan took her hand and gave it a little squeeze.

"Everything, okay?" he asked.

Could he really be that oblivious to the chaos running through her?

"No, it's not okay," she snapped. For one, she was still so angry about how things had gone down with Shane just now. And for two, her hand in Ryan's. She removed her fingers from his. "That feels weird."

"Weird?"

"Yes, weird." Her annoyance opened the floodgate. "So freaking weird that every fiber in my body is screaming, *No.*"

"Jeez, Kris, don't hold back on my account."

And there was another thing, too. . .

"You shouldn't have kissed me like that in front of everyone the other day," she said, fighting against the memory of Ryan's wet lips against hers. *What if Shane really had seen him kiss her?* "You acted like I was your property. There for the taking."

"But that was my grand gesture!" Ryan stared at her, looking stricken. He ran his fingers through his hair. "You're not sounding like yourself, Kris. You've changed."

Damn right she had.

"What do you expect? That I just accept you brushing me off for Zoey and come running back? You knew how I felt about you. You knew I wanted us to be together. But you always came up with a reason not to."

"Okay, I screwed up. I'm sorry. You know how stressed out I've been with Mom and—"

"Yeah, and if Zoey had listened to your troubles, you'd be taking her out for a meal tonight instead of me."

She'd said it flippantly, but she knew immediately she was correct. "That's why you didn't take it further with her, isn't it?" Krista said. "Zoey wasn't interested in your problems, huh?"

Something uncomfortable flickered in Ryan's eyes moments before he looked to the ground. *So she was right.* But what was the point in trudging through all this now? Krista had a whole list of why she and Ryan were wrong for each other. And although she'd seen a different angle to him, this wasn't the only reason she wasn't jumping feet first into a relationship with him.

She wanted Shane.

And, god, how she wished she could've run into his arms just now! But that wasn't Ryan's fault.

"Look, Ry, let's just be friends, okay? We were good as friends."

"Friends? Wow, cool." Sarcasm dripped off his words. He dug his hands into his pockets and looked to his feet.

Cocking her head, Krista studied his sullen face. "You know, I realized last week that I've been chasing the wrong dream. And that's what I think you're doing too."

"Now I'm a wrong dream? Gee, this romantic evening I had planned is just getting better and better."

"Aw, c'mon Ryan." She couldn't help but laugh, which seemed to deflate him even more. *Man, he was good at sulking.* "You don't want romance with me. Be honest, it's never worked that way between us. That's why we're having this discussion instead of wild sex with each other."

His head snapped up, his eyebrows wrinkled. *Wild sex? Eh?* She could practically see her words in a thought bubble above his head.

"I never saw you as the wild sex kinda gal."

"Exactly. The two of us having sex of any kind hasn't ever entered your mind, has it?" And she knew she was right when he looked to his feet again. "Doesn't that tell you something about us?"

An emotional crutch. . . Shane had certainly been right about that. And deep down, Krista had always been aware of the lack of passion between her and Ryan. It was just that the draw of that steady, long-lasting relationship she'd always craved had been too strong. But if there was one thing that she'd discovered about herself in the Rockies, it was that she wanted—*no, deserved*—a man who gave her everything. Who made her *feel* everything. Friendship and love, sizzle and sex, comfort and contentment. She wanted to feel floaty and untethered but still part of something special. Something unique and solid and exciting.

Something like she'd started with Shane.

The Seawall Path to Stanley Park. . .

If there was one thing Krista had learned from her misguided crush on Ryan, it was not to sit around and wait for things to happen. And from split pants to hiding in a bush, to crying like a heartbroken fool, she'd embarrassed herself so much in front of Shane already, what the hell else did she have to lose?

She started to run.

"Where are you going?" Ryan shouted behind her.

"To chase the right dream!"

·♥·♥·♥·♥·♥·

SHANE CLEARED THE CURB in one long stride.

What the hell was he doing?

And where the hell had all these pedestrians come from? Why so many people in his way? Swerving and dodging, he sprinted back to the aquatics center.

Back to Krista.

She was probably long gone by now. On her date with Ryan.

But Shane had to know for sure. He'd had enough of being a coward—and he'd had enough of letting what Fiona had done rule his future. Wasn't she even the whole reason why he'd devised his new life plan?

This whole past year, he'd been too afraid to step away from his strict regime of training, studying, and keeping away from women. But that was before he'd got to know Krista. Got to know her sweet and kick-assy ways. She was open and warmhearted, honest and funny, and kind.

And the heat between them had been off the charts.

Last week, they'd started *something* worth fighting for. He saw that now.

So what if Ryan had kissed her? The game wasn't over yet. Not until he heard the words *I don't want you, Shane* come straight out of Krista's mouth.

Pushing harder, he took his chance with a gap in the traffic, crossed the street—and that's when he saw her.

She was running.

Running towards him!

"You're the biggest jerk I know, Shane McDermit!" she called out breathlessly, but despite her words, there was no anger in her eyes—just. . . excitement and exhilaration, like when she'd reached the top of a mountain.

Shane stopped in front of her, his chest heaving, his heart soaring. *Why wasn't she with Ryan?*

"So, as I was saying"—Krista swiped at a strand of hair that had stuck to her lip gloss—"you're a jerk."

"You ran just to tell me that?" he asked, biting back a smile. Her hair was a mess, her cheeks red from her run. She looked adorable. And—miracle of all miracles—she was here. With him! Not Ryan.

"I like you Shane." Krista took a deep breath and squeezed her eyes shut, like she was just about to jump off a cliff. "I want us to date. And Ryan kissed *me* the other day. I was ambushed. I would've explained, but you were such a hotheaded idiot."

"I know."

Then, sucking in more air, she added, "And you wanna know what else you are?"

"A coward?"

"Yep. Like, *really* spineless. So, you got hurt. You gonna let that ruin the rest of your life?"

"No."

"And are you. . ." Krista's eyes flew open, as if his words had only just reached her. "You agree with me?"

He nodded. "Especially with the jerk and hotheaded idiot parts."

At that, she ran into his arms. Shane caught her, swooped her up off her feet and kissed her, knowing he'd never be able to get enough of her. When he pulled back, he gazed into her lovely, sparkling eyes.

"I'm sorry I took off the way I did. I'm sorry I left you," he said. His damn insecurities had got the better of him that day.

But none of that seemed to matter now. Not when Krista was back in his arms.

She grabbed his face and smacked a scorching kiss on his lips. "I want you, Shane McDermit."

And damn if he didn't want her back.

"I've missed you so much, Krista Gervais."

They kissed again, that Rocky Mountain heat stirred and whipped up the fireball that he'd been too scared to hold. But now he grabbed it, lost himself in it—man alive, he even heard bells and whistles and—

"Move out of the way, love birds! Go get a room!"

Shane and Krista jolted apart. The bells and whistles were real. They were standing in the middle of the cycle lane, and his hands were up her T-shirt, fondling her breasts.

"We're gonna get arrested," Krista said, laughing. She readjusted her clothes and tugged him away to the beach. "So, um. . . where do we go from here?"

To the large double bed in his apartment—but he knew that wasn't what Krista meant.

"This is where I wish I had a crystal ball," Shane said, gazing down at their entwined fingers. Would he and Krista last the distance or were they only destined for a few hot weeks together?

And did he really need to know the answer?

"I want to see where this thing we've started goes," he said.

"Me too." Krista looked up from their joined hands. "I want to see where this trail we're on will lead us."

And when she kissed him again, Shane no longer needed to know the answers to his future.

The fun would be in finding out all by themselves.

Epilogue

SIX MONTHS LATER...

Flames crackled softly in the fireplace. As Shane added another log and stoked the fire, Krista enjoyed the play of muscles flickering across his bare back, his skin aglow with warm orange light.

"So, your folks back home won't be mad at us?" she asked, gathering the fluffy blanket close to her chest as she curled up on the plush fireside rug. "I bet your sister will have a go at me."

"No more than yours had a go at me earlier."

Krista giggled. She could still hear Lisa's squeal when she'd called her to tell her the news. She hadn't been pleased—and neither had Mom—but they'd both soon come round when Shane assured them there would be a big party. In fact, two big parties. One in Canada, and one in Australia.

Everything had happened so fast today. One minute, she and Shane had been strolling through the snow-covered streets of Banff—window shopping, grabbing a bite to eat and drink, like couples do—then the next, they were at the Banff Registry, waiting for their marriage license to be issued.

An hour after that, they were with an officiant at their cute Rocky Mountain Lodge with the two witnesses he'd managed to conjure up, and hey presto—she and Shane were husband and wife.

"No regrets?" he asked her now as he joined her on the rug.

Krista shifted to make room for him, lifting the blanket so he could come underneath. His eyebrow arched as his gaze skimmed along her naked body. Well, naked apart from the gold wedding band she wore on her left ring finger. It matched the one he wore on his. That's what had started this crazy idea. They'd passed a jeweler's store window, had both stopped to look at the rings—and then at each other.

"I haven't had a single regret since that day I chased after you," she said, snuggling against his chest.

These past six months had been the happiest of her life. Being with Shane always felt like the beginning of a great adventure, and days like today were no exception.

They were both still riding high after Shane had won gold in the 100m freestyle at the Pan Pacific Championships last week, with Mikey Adams coming a very close second. To celebrate, Shane had suggested they hop on a flight to Banff to experience the winter wonderland of the Rockies for a few days. "We can thaw out in Sydney," he'd said. Next week, they'd be spending Christmas with his family in Australia.

Which reminded her that now was the time to tell Shane about her decision.

She raised her head off his chest and looked straight into his eyes. "I'm handing in my resignation at the aquatics center."

"What? No, you—"

She pressed her fingers against his lips. "It's not what I want anymore."

Shane stared at her for a long time. It was one of those stares that she used to find so hard to read. But now, she could pick out the warmth in his eyes and the softness around his lips, and she knew he was processing everything that her words meant.

"I want to set up my own practice and work for myself. In Australia," she added firmly.

So far, they'd managed to dance around the subject of which country they should live in. They'd agreed to a long-distance relationship for the next year—one reason why eloping today had felt so right—but now that Krista was all snuggled up in Shane's arms, she never wanted to leave.

Neither of them were looking forward to long months apart anyway, because after their three-week-long vacation in Sydney came to an end, Shane wouldn't be able to return to Vancouver until after the Olympics in July. And then in September, his first sports consultancy contract at Darwin University would begin. The whole of next year was mapped out for him. Krista loved him too much to ask him to give it all up, and she knew he loved her too much to ask her to change her career plans, too.

"What's the point in wasting our time together and living apart?" she said. "I want to be with you, Shane. I can still travel to the Olympics with Team Canada, but after that, I want to work alongside you in Australia."

Gently, he cupped her face and hovered his lips just above hers.

"You're sure?" he whispered.

"You bet I am," she whispered back. "You don't get to be rid of me so easily."

"So, I'm stuck with you, huh?"

"Yeah." Smiling, Krista chinked her wedding band against his, and as the fire crackled gently beside them, Shane planted a sweet little kiss on her lips.

It was a promise, forever binding, that no matter what steep climbs and obstacles lay ahead, they would always find the trail and keep on it together.

WANT TO READ ANOTHER FEEL-GOOD ROMANCE LIKE THIS?

Check out my other books!
And find out who Mikey meets on his unexpected trip to visit Shane and Krista in Australia.
His story is told in *Her Outback Driver*.

www.giuliaskye.com

Her Outback Driver

Another photo shoot. . . Another TV show. . .
I don't want this anymore!

When former Olympic champion, Michael Adams—now Canada's hottest reality TV star—insults his fake showbiz wife on social media, he jumps on the first flight to Australia to escape the ensuing scandal. Desperate to experience ordinary life again—if only for a few weeks—he becomes "Adam"; just another tourist exploring the dusty Outback trails in a beat up truck. But with a reward out for his safe return and his fame's nasty habit of catching up with him when he least expects, Adam needs a better disguise... and he's just found one.

Tired of lies and liars, British backpacker Evie Blake is taking a year out of her busy London life, looking for adventure to heal her broken heart. So when the hot Canadian she meets at the campground offers to drive her through Western Australia's wild Kimberley region, she grabs the chance, unaware he has the world out looking for him.

He's just a down-on-his-luck traveler, right?

But when hot days turn into even hotter nights, how long does Adam have before Evie discovers who he really is?

Author's Note: False identity. Road trip romance. Smart banter. Guy on the run. Stunning Australian scenery. Al fresco you-know-what. Cinnamon roll hero. Cute and strong heroine who sweeps hero off his feet. Occasional F-bombs.
Pace: Zippy, with a few twists along the way.
Steam Level: Hot with a purpose.
Feels: ALL.OF.THEM.

FIND OUT MORE ON GIULIA SKYE'S WEBSITE
www.giuliaskye.com

Her Outback Driver - Extract

ADAM ORDERED A FRUIT juice packed with crushed ice and watched Miss Bug Eyes while he waited for his change.

She was sitting on the edge of a leather sofa next to the floor-to-ceiling window. He'd first taken her for a college graduate, but she looked older now, her huge bush-baby eyes crinkling at the corners as she scowled at her phone. He pegged her at twenty-eight, thirty at a very hard push, just a few years younger than his thirty-three.

The woman at the campground had told him her name was Evie, but the name was too feminine—too cute—for someone who looked like her, particularly when she frowned like she was doing now. She wasn't ugly, not by a long stretch, just plain in a nothing-to-write-home-about kind of way. Perfect for a travel budding?

Certain that he'd shaken off the experience in the surplus store, Adam walked over to her.

"Why the long face?" he said, dumping himself next to her on the sofa. "Did someone ignore another of your signs?"

He'd made her jump, but her voice sounded just as haughty as it did yesterday. "Oh, it's you." She gave him a tight smile. "I didn't recognize you with your clothes on."

Which was a load of crap. He'd seen the way she'd stared at him across the campground. "Yeah, about that. Pretty unfortunate incident, eh?" And because he didn't want to suggest they become travel buddies only to realize out on the highway that she knew who he was, Adam pushed for signs of recognition. "You could make a lot of money selling that story."

Her quick bark of laughter had him raising one eyebrow and she swallowed back words sounding a lot like, In your dreams. Adam hid his smile. She didn't have a clue about him.

"So I'm guessing you're from England," he said.

"You guess right." She cast those eyes over him. "And I'm guessing you're from America. Whereabouts?"

"Edmonton."

"Edmonton?" She frowned. "But isn't that in Canada?"

"Yeah."

"Oh."

She turned back to her phone.

Right. He'd never been the funniest guy in the room, but he'd hoped that attempt at humor was worthy of at least a half-smile. Instead her quick dismissal told him he'd just come across as an idiot—an idiot who didn't hold her attention for long. Her phone buzzed with an incoming message and he lost her.

Adam drained his juice, crunched on an ice cube and tapped the bottom of her grubby backpack with the toe of his running shoe, making the point that—hello?—he was still sitting beside her. "You leaving Broome today? I heard you were looking for a ride to Darwin along the Gibb River Road."

That got her attention.

She glanced up, her eyes wide. "Lorraine said she'd told you."

Lorraine? Right. The campground woman. "Yeah, I didn't think much more of it until I saw you here." He nodded through the window toward his truck, hoping his teeth weren't grinding together. "I'm looking for a travel buddy to share costs and adventures."

·♥·♥·♥·♥·♥·

HEARING THE WORDS SHE'D written for her ad, Evie angled her head and clocked the dusty truck across the street. A big beast of a four-wheel drive with chunky tires and a snorkel exhaust fitted to the side of the cab, meaning true outback business.

"I'm sorry," her pulse quickened, "did you say you were looking to car-share along the Gibb River Road?"

"Yeah, I'm leaving for Derby now. Wanna ride?"

Adrenaline pumped through her, like she should grab this opportunity or be forever stuck. She thought of Lorraine as a young woman jumping on a boat in Somalia moments before the military descended to close the port. Evie now felt like taking that same leap, the last of Zac's messages burning a hole in her hand and her heart.

We didn't tell you before because we didn't want to ruin your travels.

And there it was again. We. Zac and Teagan, not Zac and Evie as it had always been. We. Zac snuggling next to Teagan, her full breasts nursing their newborn son. Just then that old dream of bumping through the outback in a trail of red dust, holding on to her seat, hair flying wild, flashed before her. It was so bright and bold it already felt like a memory, blowing away that image of we that was lodged painfully in her mind like barbed wire.

Wanna ride?

Yes! Hell, yes, she did.

WANT TO KEEP READING?

Find out more at www.giuliaskye.com

The Summer of Sebastian

There's been a mistake...

Olympic athlete Sebastian Clarke has six weeks to repair the damage to his reputation or lose the funding he needs to finally win that gold. Working as a sports ambassador in England for the summer is the perfect way to prove to his sponsors that he's still their wholesome hero, and to seal the deal, he's hired a sweet university librarian to pose as his girlfriend. Cassie is nothing like the Las Vegas showgirls the media stirred the truth with last month, but when she turns up late for their first meeting, Seb doesn't expect to find her with a large plate of food in her hands and a startled look in her eyes.

Are you freaking kidding me?

Computer-geek Helen Hobbs only borrowed Cassie's access badge to snaffle a free meal—just her damn luck to be caught red-handed by a hunk of a man who immediately spouts on about contracts, rules and schedules. Helen tells him he's made a mistake, but a journalist hungry for trash on the disgraced sporting star is already hot on their tail. So, maybe now isn't a good time to tell Sebastian she's on probation...

nor that she's under police surveillance for accidentally working with the UK's most wanted cyber criminal.

Forced to hire Helen as his fake-girlfriend, can Sebastian keep this trouble magnet in line before she ruins his career?

They have a contract. . .

But who will be the first to break the rules?

Author's Note: Fake relationship. Opposites attract. Snappy, hot banter. Girl in danger. Uptight hero depriving himself of fun times until. . . he doesn't. Beautiful English countryside. Kick-ass, trouble-magnet heroine who keeps pushing the hero's buttons. Occasional F-bombs.
Steam Level: Hot and with a purpose.
Pace: Nail-biting.
Feels: ALL.OF.THEM.

FIND OUT MORE ON GIULIA SKYE'S WEBSITE:

www.giuliaskye.com

The Summer of
Sebastian - Extract

IF THOSE CRAZY LONG legs of hers weren't a distraction, the nipples puckering under the thin material of that cheap dress certainly were. Seb diverted his gaze from the two protruding buds as he slid in next to Helen on the backseat.

He'd just spoken to Mikey to explain, using the same bullshit that Brenda had heard earlier, about why Cassie was now called Helen. Seb had apologized for the bad timing of his revelation—jeez, but his new boss had other things on his mind right now—but Mikey had been understanding, and Seb had vowed to make this year's campaign a success. He'd do everything in his power to make things right, which included pretending that this stranger beside him was the love of his life.

"So what really happened to Cassie?" Helen asked as the driver pulled away from the curb.

Seb's gaze drifted again to the dress shrink-wrapped over her long, slender body, her breasts like two ripe plums below her deep collar line. The clothes he'd seen her wear so far had done nothing for her willowy figure, but this? It left nothing to the imagination.

Seb tugged at his collar. "It's like you called it. She had a family emergency." When Helen wriggled her dress down from where it had ridden up her bare thighs, Seb turned to the window. "Cassie's father had a stroke yesterday in France, she flew to be with him and won't be back until September."

"Wow. That is scary."

"Yeah, but sounds like he's gonna be fine though."

"I was referring to me being right, but I'm glad he's okay." She fussed with her dress again. "So, tonight I'm being me, but I'm still to carry on telling people I write poetry because that's what the scary lady thinks?"

"She's called Brenda." And Seb had to agree that she could be scary, but since learning he was in love, Brenda had softened considerably toward him. "I figured you writing poetry was a white lie we could live with. Lots of people have aspirations to be writers, but please don't bring it up unless you have to. If anyone asks, you're taking time off work to help me out at the Get Living headquarters."

"Putting my career on hold to boost yours?" Helen's lips puckered. "That makes me sound like the little woman at home."

"Don't get on your high horse about it. How else are we gonna explain you working in the yard? Those reporters today, including Grice, have no reason to believe you're on probation, and I'm assuming you haven't shouted it from the rooftops."

"No, just my family and a friend know."

That was something, at least. "And that love you spoke so readily about earlier? You're giving it a chance by being fully supportive of my work." Again, his gaze dipped past her glossy lips to her barely-there cleavage. Recalling her Byte Me tattoo, Seb frowned. "What work did you do for that boss you tried to steal from?"

"Ex-boss, and that money was mine so I wasn't stealing it."

"You were if you had to break in to his apartment." Seb strived for calm. "You didn't answer my question."

"I design and maintain websites," Helen said, then tilted her chin toward him. "I was reading about you yesterday."

Avoidance. What a surprise. That didn't bode well for what he'd find out about her, but as soon as tonight's dinner was over, he'd make it his mission to find out every damn thing about Helen Hobbs so he could mitigate any other disasters before they happened. "Did you come across anything interesting about me?"

"Lots of things." She crossed her legs. The hem of her dress rode up to her crotch. Sweet lord. Please be wearing panties? The very last thing he needed were indecent photographs splashed across the internet if she tripped in those heels. "They're all very pretty and makes me wonder why you didn't know what she looked like."

Seb blinked as Helen waited expectantly. Too distracted by hemlines and crotches, he'd clearly missed something. "What who looked like?"

"Cassie. Why didn't you have a picture of her?"

"Looks aren't important to me."

"Bollocks."

Bollocks? That sounded a lot like bullshit. "Okay, I'll confess. I was halfway across the Atlantic, there wasn't time, and Jimmy's description was good enough for me."

"Very slapdash for someone so organized."

Huh. "I admit my original plan sucked, but I can assure you"—Seb motioned between them—"this one sucks even more. But fear not, under the current circumstances, I've devised a new plan, the theme being love conquers all."

She sniffed the air. "I smell flowery bullshit."

"I've taken some very recent lessons." Seb gazed out of the window again. The Friday evening sidewalks were busy, full of couples strolling hand in hand, pointing at menus in restaurant windows. "You were right earlier. Brenda, nor anyone else, will be fooled for long if we don't do a good job of acting like we're in love. So, I'm gonna do all it takes to make our relationship believable, starting with us living together. From tonight. Do you have a spare room for me at your place?"

She gasped. "You want to live with me?"

"No, I don't want to. I need to." Seb couldn't let Helen go tonight without knowing where she lived. For all he knew, the address she'd written on the salary form could be as fake as their relationship—particularly, as his Google Maps search earlier had the location icon pointing to the middle of a field. "Love conquers all, remember? And I'm conquering the fact that you could potentially ruin my career."

WANT TO KEEP READING?

Find out more at www.giuliaskye.com

Acknowledgments

Thank you to my wonderful beta readers—Howard Diamond, Silvia Pascale and Jacqueline Stewart—you are always so very kind reading my early drafts and telling me you like them! I am very lucky to have your support.

Thank you also to my critique partner, Kathy Strobos. I am so grateful to you have as a friend and colleague!

Printed in Great Britain
by Amazon

36723624R00118